CARELESS

Also by Anne Cassidy

Blood Money
Innocent
The Dead House

CARELESS

ANNE CASSIDY

Hodder
Children's
Books

A division of Hachette Children's Books

ISBN: 978 0 340 93227 8

Typeset in Baskerville by Avon DataSet Ltd,
Bidford-on-Avon, Warwickshire

Printed and bound in Great Britain by
Clays Ltd, St Ives plc

The paper and board used in this paperback by Hodder Children's
Books are natural recyclable products made from wood grown
in sustainable forests. The manufacturing processes conform to the
environmental regulations of the country of origin.

Hodder Children's Books
a division of Hachette Children's Books
338 Euston Road, London NW1 3BH
An Hachette UK company

Part One

Lost

1

The first night was bad enough. Alone, in the dark, Nicky's resentment was like a great weight that bore down on him. He lay back, closed his eyes and tried to breathe deeply but the hurt of it, the *injustice* of it made him toss and turn until his bed was wrecked and his pillows flung about the room. Later, in the blackest part of the night, he got angry. He fought back. He punched and kicked and threw himself about. That's why things got broken up in his room. His radio clock, his Walkman, his books, his desk, the pictures on his walls.

It just made things worse. Next day people started to stick their noses in. The care workers, the nurse, the doctor. Everyone got worried and Trevor, his new social worker, made a point of knocking lightly on his door at regular intervals saying, 'Everything all right, Nicky?'

Nothing was right. That was the trouble.

He had to pretend it was, though, otherwise he wouldn't be left alone. Daytime was easy. That first day, just after Lesley's letter came, he'd tried to shake it off, to bury himself in other things. It was possible, in Crystal House, to find other people to talk to. He used the computer and went on the internet and found music websites to trespass on. He went out and bought a magazine and looked idly round the shops, pricing up the music decks and looking at the black vinyls. During the day, the world always seemed like a calm place where nothing too bad could go wrong. It was possible then to see the letter in a different light. *Dear Nicky*, it said, *I'm writing because I don't know if I'm going to see you again.*

It was a goodbye note. That was all. Somebody was leaving him and they were clearing up loose ends. He could even see a funny side to it. The first ever letter he had received that hadn't been typed on official stationery. He had opened it with delight only to find that the nice handwriting concealed a hard truth. It was a bad joke and he had laughed grimly at it.

Lesley had been ill and didn't know if she was going to get better. She'd had to find some notepaper and a pen and write the words down, like a sort of confession.

You've not had a happy life, I know . . . I feel responsible . . .

In daylight, when he read the letter, it didn't sound so bad. Sentence after sentence of neat writing, explaining about Nicky's life and why it had been messed up. Lesley had said it was her fault. She had owned up. He felt quite sorry for her.

But on that second night, when the lights went off in the corridors of Crystal House and Nicky stepped into his empty room, he felt more alone than he ever had in his entire life. The door clicked behind him and it was as if he was standing in a boat in the middle of a silent ocean, the water flat and deep and dangerous.

He let Lesley's letter drop out of his hand, only paper and words he knew, but he wanted it to float away from him so he'd never have to read it again. It stayed there on the floor by his foot, a heavy weight that would drag him down. He snatched it up and took it to the window, struggling to open the catch so that he could throw it out, let the wind carry it away.

It wouldn't open though. He was poised with this bit of paper, wanting to do something dramatic and momentous, to flush these words out of his life once and for all, and he couldn't turn the handle. He stood hopelessly for a moment feeling the laughter bubble out of his mouth, his fingers hanging pathetically on the catch.

Why him? Did he have so little power over his own life that he couldn't even open a window?

There was no clear answer. That's why he turned and looked at his room with rage. He pulled the television from the shelf and rammed it into the glass panes, his voice tearing out of him, his hands and arms shaking with anger. The sound of voices and footsteps running along the corridor stopped him, made him stand to attention, biting his lips with irritation. He'd done it again. Now they would be all over him, Trevor and the others. When they charged into his room he avoided looking at them, his eyes dropping to the ground searching for the letter. Seeing it, by the foot of his bed, he picked it up and shoved it back into his pocket. He couldn't afford to lose it. It was his proof and somebody would have to pay.

Dear Nicky . . . You are unhappy because of decisions I made, choices I took. If I had done things differently things may have been better . . .

It was too late for Lesley though. She would never be able to pay for what she had done.

2

The death was expected but the loss was still hard.

They may only have weeks, the doctors had said, so they'd taken her mum home from the hospital in her dad's van. The back had been full of tins of paint and electric tools but they'd cleared a place for Chloe to sit while her mum and dad sat in the front. It had been like an escape, the three of them barely speaking above a whisper, the van speeding along the dual carriageway towards home. It was a wet day and Chloe focused on the windscreen wipers going from left to right, clearing the glass only to have it blurred again by a thousand tiny darts of rain a second later.

They would have to make the most of the time that was left. All three of them.

A hospital bed arrived and was put together in the back dining room where the French doors opened out on to the garden. It fitted in alongside the folded-up table, the armchairs and the Welsh dresser that her mum had bought and renovated some years before. Her dad pulled the hi-fi out of the corner of the living room and set it up on the other side of the bed where her mum could reach it. She wanted her CDs; jazz music that usually gave Chloe a headache.

Her dad went out especially and bought a small TV with a sleep button.

'Look, Lesley,' he'd said, 'if you fall asleep while watching, the set will turn itself off.'

Her mum had given a tired smile.

'That's handy,' she'd said. 'If I kick the bucket while I'm watching, it'll save on electricity!'

Her dad's eyes had filled up with tears at this and Chloe felt her own throat hot and sore as if it were tangled up with barbed wire.

'Come on! We're not going to sit round and cry the whole time!'

Her mum had been adamant that the weeping would have to stop. They tried. For a while it was difficult, each of them tiptoeing around, blinking back tears, turning away to pat a cushion or collect a magazine. When things got too much there was always the kettle to fill, the dishes to wash, the rubbish bin to empty.

Then things settled and Chloe and her mum and dad adapted to the new life that was centred around the back dining room. It was May so the doors could be opened most mornings as the nurse came on the first of her visits. They had breakfast together, the three of them: Chloe sitting on the edge of the hospital bed balancing her bowl of cornflakes; her dad cross-legged on the floor, his big workboots taking up all the space, his plate on a pile of books; her mum with a small plate of scrambled eggs and toast fingers.

Then Chloe went to school.

'I want you to go,' her mum said. 'How are me and Dad ever meant to have any time alone if you're always here?'

The nurse, Geraldine, a small Irish lady who wore a heavy cross on a chain round her neck, tutted loudly.

'Now, Lesley, I've told you about that!'

Chloe knew it was all jokes but she put her uniform on and filled her rucksack and set off at the same time every day. As she was leaving one day she stood for a moment at the front door listening to Geraldine's chatter and her mum and dad's voices and felt a great dark hole opening up in front of her. She seemed to lose her balance as if at the edge of a precipice but held on firmly to the doorknob until she heard her mum's voice again, soft and scratchy, agreeing with something that Geraldine had said.

Every afternoon she got off the bus and wondered what was waiting for her at home. She'd use the pelican crossing and walk slowly across the road looking closely at her surroundings as she went. The off-licence, the betting shop, the chemist. Then she'd go the long way round, passing the entrance to the tube station, where the minicabs were all parked at crazy angles, their drivers leaning on the bonnets, languidly waiting for fares.

Her own street was long and tree-lined and some days she counted the steps from the beginning to her own front door. Six hundred. Sometimes, if she stretched her legs, she could make it five hundred and sixty: more often than not she forgot to count after she got past a couple of hundred.

Every day she wondered if her mum would be awake when she got in. She said those words to herself: *Will she be awake?* but really, deep inside, she knew that she meant something quite different.

She used her own key and always shouted out *I'm home!* as soon as she got in. Then they would have their tea together and her dad would go off for a while leaving the two of them to watch the soaps on the tiny TV. Afterwards Geraldine or some other nurse would come by and get her mum ready for the night. The medicine had to be taken: pills at first, then a drip that was attached to her mum's arm.

There were visitors during those weeks. Her mum's workmates and some family friends. Her grandmother came; a big blonde-haired woman whom Chloe didn't see often. When the visit was over she gave Chloe a crushing hug, her shoulders shaking with emotion. Her dad drove her to the station and waited with her until her Suffolk train came. Her mum had seemed agitated afterwards so Chloe had taken the china out of the Welsh dresser and the two of them cleaned each piece carefully. Afterwards her mum dozed for a long time.

At night-times, when it was just getting dark, she and her mum would watch next door's cat, a skinny, spiteful creature, walking across the back wall, stopping every few feet to listen hard at something.

'You could lace your boots with that cat,' her mum often said.

The following week the drip was taken away and her mum was given injections.

A couple of days later, as Chloe got off the bus from school, a terrible feeling took hold of her. She looked at the traffic streaming past, at the shops and the tube station and the end of her street. Everything was the same and yet the world seemed suddenly a different place. She found herself running at first, dodging between the cars and sidestepping the pedestrians. She caught the eye of the man at the paper stand outside the tube and he seemed to look sympathetically at her as though he knew something that she didn't.

Turning into her street the noise of the main road died away and she took each step quickly until in the distance her house loomed up ahead of her. Then she slowed down. It was better not to rush. If she took her time she could add minutes to her journey; she could hold back the moment when the front door opened and she would shout *I'm home* and no one would answer.

When she finally stepped into the hallway her mum was gone.

It was so sudden, Geraldine, her dad said to the nurse as she left for the last time. *I didn't think it would be as quick as that.*

For a couple of days Chloe and her dad spent a lot of time in the back dining room. They left the French doors open until it got too cold, played the CDs and watched the tiny TV. They ate off plates on trays and stayed in their clothes, not getting changed or washing. Before going up to bed Chloe looked out into the moonlit garden, as quiet and still as a cemetery. Somewhere, in another garden, she pictured the bootlace cat restlessly prowling about.

After the second day her dad became businesslike. He stayed upstairs for what seemed like hours and came down washed and clean in his suit and tie and said he was going to the undertaker's first then the solicitor's. He told Chloe he'd be back later to take her to register the death.

When he was gone Chloe lay on the hospital bed. She buried her face in her mum's pillows and stayed like that for a long time.

The letters of sympathy came every day. They slid through the letterbox and fluttered to the floor. Chloe picked them up and piled them on to the hall table. Sometimes they were addressed to *Mr Michael Cozens* or more often *The Cozens family*.

'More letters of condolence,' her dad said, on the morning of the funeral. He picked up the pile of unopened envelopes and flicked through.

'We'll let the dust settle before we open up these, OK?' he said, giving her a hug.

The funeral was for eleven o'clock but a lot of people came round to the house an hour or so before. Her dad answered the front door and greeted people jovially as though it was some kind of party that they had come for. Chloe found herself leaning against a wall, pressing her shoulder blades into the plaster as though she was physically holding it up. Around her there was a buzz of conversation, the clink of cups and saucers, her dad talking to people, his voice almost cheerful.

When the funeral cars arrived Chloe looked round to see her gran burst into hoarse sobs. Her blonde hair was styled and looked like it had been done at the hairdresser's. *Are you going anywhere nice?* she imagined the hairdresser saying. Her gran looked like she was going to say something to her but instead she blew her nose in a large white handkerchief. Chloe stayed where she was as the mourners put their drinks down and made their way out into the brilliant sunshine. She counted them. Nineteen people had come to the house. There would be more in the church.

For a moment she didn't know if she could move. The wall behind her felt heavy and she had this ridiculous idea that if she stepped away it would topple and fall into the room.

Her dad's face appeared at the door and he held his hand out beckoning for her to join him. Using her elbows she pushed herself away and reached out to him.

A couple of women had just come downstairs from the

toilet and they were following her. She heard one of them talking about the weather.

'A sunny day for a funeral. That's bad luck,' the woman said.

'Don't be ridiculous,' her companion said, shushing her friend.

Bad luck. Chloe almost smiled. She and her dad had just lost Mum. How could their luck be any worse?

3

Nicky stood stiffly back against the wall of a derelict house and watched the funeral cars drive off. He let his rucksack fall off his shoulder and on to the ground. There were other people standing in the sunshine, their arms crossed, their faces long; neighbours who had come out of their houses to show their respect to the coffin.

Nicky let the saliva collect in his mouth and then spat it on to the pavement. A couple of the nearby people tutted and whispered to each other but he didn't care. Using his thumb he rubbed at a small hole in the knee of his jeans. One by one the onlookers disappeared into their houses and he was alone in the street opposite Lesley Cozens's house. Except it wasn't hers any more because she was dead. It probably belonged to her husband and her wimpish-looking daughter.

Nicky shoved his hands into the pockets of his jeans. In one of them was a folded-up envelope. He pulled it out. It was a light blue colour and a few days ago it had held the letter that had dropped into his life as casually as a hand grenade. He flattened it out and saw his name and address written neatly on it, *Nicky Nelson, Crystal*

House, Brook Road, Walthamstow, E17.

She hadn't addressed the letter herself. Inside it had been a second envelope with his name on. Someone else had posted it and they had shoved it into some odd-looking envelope that had been hanging around.

Why should she? She had her *own family* to care for. He was just a boy that she had been paid to look after. A social work caseload. A set of details in a brown file that she had had to wade through.

He walked across the street and up to the gate in front of the house. It was on a corner, deserted, as quiet as a cemetery. The front garden was full of green shrubs and there were climbing plants up the wall and around the window. He moved along a bit and looked through the glass. There were no net curtains and he could see into the living room. A long sofa and a giant plant that looked like a palm tree. The walls were covered in pictures and there were shelves of books.

This was where his old social worker had lived. How different it was to Crystal House. Nicky found himself fidgeting with a loose brick that was on the garden wall, pulling at it until it came free and holding it tightly to his chest.

He pictured Lesley Cozens standing by the door of her car the last time he ever saw her. Months ago it seemed. She'd been wearing her usual leather jacket. *You'll have to have that jacket surgically removed!* he'd joked with her. They'd known each other a while then.

She'd waved at him. She was having a couple of weeks off for an operation she'd said, then she'd be back to keep her eye on him. She'd told him to work hard in his 'A's and not to stay out late at night.

He never saw her again. She'd been sucked back into her own family and he'd been left alone. All there was for him was a letter in a blue envelope. It had wounded him, he couldn't deny it. Which was odd because after leaving the Marshalls he had thought nothing could ever hurt him so much again.

Nicky squeezed the brick in his hand until it chafed against his skin. The Marshall family. He remembered that gripping pain across his guts as he cleared his things out of the chest of drawers that was supposed to be his. Lesley had been late coming to collect him and he'd taken a nail and used the waiting time to scratch the skin on his arm back and forth across until it was crimson with blood. They'd been shocked and he'd laughed but inside the soreness was hot and he'd thought his skin was on fire.

He looked down at his arm and saw the red scars as though someone had scribbled on his skin. He noticed the brick that his hand was holding and wondered for a moment where it had come from. Then he saw the gap in the wall where he'd pulled it out. He shouldn't have done that. The wall looked spoilt. It would upset people.

It wouldn't bother Lesley. She wouldn't feel anything because she was dead. She had made decisions for him and then deserted him just like everyone else. He felt light-headed for a moment and had to concentrate to keep standing upright. He found himself gripping the rough edges of the brick, his front teeth biting into his bottom lip. He wanted to say something, to shout out, to tell people what had happened.

But no words came, just a choking sob.

The brick seemed to fly through the air of its own accord. In seconds the living-room window shattered and the glass cascaded into the garden. The sound shocked him and he stood looking at it for a few moments, tasting the blood from his lip. Then he turned and walked away.

4

Chloe found her blue envelope when they started to open up the sympathy letters a week later. The contents were written on white paper but the envelope was a light blue colour, quite large as though it had once been used for a greetings card. Afterwards she came to think of it as the *blue letter*.

It was addressed to *Miss Chloe Cozens* and it must have been placed amid the pile of cards and letters that had come around the time of the funeral. Her dad had made a collection of them in a drawer and said that they would look at them when they felt better.

It was hard to know, though, exactly when they would feel better.

He'd begun to sort through them after a phone call from her gran in Suffolk. She had rung regularly and was keen for Chloe to go and spend some time with her. Her dad had made faces while speaking to her on the phone but Chloe was resigned to the fact that she would have to go. He handed her the letter as soon as he found it.

It was a relief to see her dad looking relaxed. She made

the most of it. It might not last, she knew. He could go for days being strong and positive and without warning he would crumple into a ball at the edge of the settee and sit with his face in the palm of his hands.

Like the day of the funeral. He'd organized the guests and made everyone feel easy and calm. He'd read a poem out at the service and had persuaded lots of people to follow them back to the house for drinks and snacks. But when he was faced with the smashed living-room window he simply folded up there and then on the pavement and had to be helped inside. A neighbour nailed hardwood over the broken glass while he went and lay down in his bedroom. The snacks sat untouched until the next morning when Chloe and her dad swept them into a black plastic sack.

She left her dad to open up the letters of condolence and went upstairs carrying a mug of tea and the blue envelope. In her room she was faced with half a dozen piles of photographs dotted around the carpet. She tutted and stepped around them until she got to her bedside table. It was probably better to get the photos into some order before she did anything else. She put the tea and the letter down and squatted on to the floor.

It was a project that she had started a few days before. They'd got out the family photographs and looked through some of them. Chloe had felt herself reduced to tears almost as soon as she'd looked at her mum's smiling face. Her dad's voice had started to break up as well and she knew then that it had been a bad idea to get the box out. She was all for packing them away but her dad took hold of the situation.

'Let's do this properly,' he said, clearing his throat. 'We'll look at each photo and have a sort of game. We have to try and remember where and when it was taken and what we'd been doing. Ten points for the one who gets it first.'

The points didn't matter and they both knew it. Chloe recognized the first one instantly.

'That was Brighton. We'd gone for the day. We'd just been in that restaurant, the one with the swirling fans on the ceiling.'

'This is Devon. You were only about three then, I think. There was this rock pool that you insisted on going to look at and you skinned the side of your foot.'

'This one was two Christmases ago. You know, when your friend from work brought his girlfriend round and Mum didn't like her. She said she . . .'

'I remember. She said the girl was just a walking bosom with big hair.'

'And you said she was just jealous.'

They both laughed and continued looking through the pictures talking about the things they had done, the three of them. After a while, when they'd only gone through a fraction of what was there, Chloe sat back against the settee and sighed. It hadn't turned out badly at all. Looking at the photos had brought her mum back to life for a few hours; her voice, her phrases, her never-ending plans and arrangements.

'These need to be sorted out,' her dad said, quietly. 'If they were in albums, in order, it would be a kind of photographic biography.'

And that was where the idea came from. Later, when she was on her own, in her bedroom, she let her dad's words replay over in her head, *A photographic biography*. What if she were to do just that? Create her mother's biography in pictures?

She began to cry but took no notice of the tears, sniffing hard and wiping her face with the back of her hand. It happened too often to stop what she was doing. It was always there, a great pool of sadness behind her eyes that weighed her down. She tried to keep the tears in, especially in front of her dad, but like an overflow of water they forced their way out. Sometimes they were like a light sprinkle of rain, a couple of sniffs and they were gone; other times they were hot and passionate, burning her cheeks and making her eyes feel raw.

She looked around at the photos. There were piles of them. On the chest of drawers sat five plastic photo albums which she'd bought. She was going to organize her mother's life: her childhood in Suffolk, her adolescence, her university days, the wedding, her life as a wife and mother and the job that she loved as a social worker. Chloe was going to sort, categorize and file until she had five books of photos which would tell a kind of story.

She sat down on her bed and noticed the blue letter. She sighed, wondering who would write a letter of condolence to *her* rather than her dad. She had had cards from friends at school and had spoken to all of them on the phone. She picked it up and carelessly tore through the paper with her thumb. A single piece of white paper was inside. It was folded in half and she opened it and read the words on the page.

I'm not sorry your mum's dead. She ruined my life.

She sat up stiffly. She let her eyes read the words over again, two or three times. A sick feeling rose in her stomach. Who would write such a thing? At this time? She stood up, the paper hanging in her hand. She had an urge to screw it up and throw it in the bin. How could anyone say something like that about her mum? Lesley Cozens, always working hard to sort out someone's problems. Never refused a phone call from work and often went out late at night to respond to some emergency to do with one of the children she worked with. She sat back on the bed with a thump and let the paper flop on to her lap. Then after a moment she picked it up and read it again. She turned the sheet over even though she knew there was nothing on the other side. She picked the envelope up and shook it, peering inside to see if there was something more.

A look of incomprehension settled on her face as she looked through a blur at the piles of photographs on the floor.

She ruined my life.

What did it mean?

Chloe folded the paper up and placed it back into the envelope. It was two weeks since her mum had died. Fourteen days. In all that time no one had said a bad word against her.

She didn't understand it and wasn't going to try.

5

Nicky lay sideways across the bed and looked around his room. Its neatness impressed him. Just a small space really but cleverly designed to house a bed, a chest of drawers, an armchair, some bookshelves, a desk and a small TV and hi-fi perched up on the wall.

The room had been recently redecorated. He had chosen the colours, maroon and black. The duvet and sheets matched and there was a rug on the floor that he had bought at IKEA on a shopping trip with Trevor. His television was new and so was the hi-fi. The replacements had been expensive but nobody had moaned at him. Damage to property was a fact of life in these places. Everyone knew that.

It was his private space. He had a key and none of the other kids or staff were allowed in there unless he wanted them. There was a master key in the caretaker's office but it was only used in emergencies. It hadn't been needed in those dark days after he got Lesley's letter because he hadn't locked the door. This had pleased Trevor. He said it was because deep down Nicky had wanted people to come in and stop him doing damage to himself.

Nicky hadn't answered, just shrugged his shoulders. It had been a while since he had done damage to himself or anyone else. He was past that. If he was angry he hit out at *things*.

In his hand was a packet of photographs that he'd taken over the last week or so. Trevor had given him the camera and told him to take pictures of the area. *Make you feel more a part of it*, he'd said, clapping Nicky on the shoulder and slipping him a couple of pound coins. He often did that. Not that Nicky was short of money. He had over three hundred pounds in his building society book plus he got a reasonable weekly allowance. But Trevor often liked to give him a few quid, something mid-week when he thought Nicky might be running short; sometimes he said he'd had a win on the horses, *but don't tell anyone*, he'd whisper conspiratorially, as if it was their little secret. Nicky wondered if Trevor was given an allowance for these little gifts. Not that he was bothered one way or another. Trevor was just doing his job; just like all the others.

He'd thought Lesley Cozens was different. When he had first set eyes on her she was running through the pouring rain down the garden path of his last but one council home. She'd been holding a plastic bag over her head to keep the rain off but it hadn't worked. Once inside the house, she had pulled it off her hair and the water had dribbled down her front, wetting her shirt. He'd offered her a towel, he remembered, from the cupboard under the stairs.

'You're Nicky, aren't you?' she'd said, shaking the drips off her head.

She was late. He'd been expecting her for almost an hour. She brought news about his placement at the Marshalls'.

'You'll like it there,' she'd said. 'They've got a son a little bit older than you. His name's Ben!'

She'd spent a long time with him, gone along on visits to the new family. Rang him regularly. Afterwards, when it had all gone wrong, she'd taken his side; even though she hadn't really understood what had happened. She stuck by me, he thought, looking out of the window at the giant trees that swayed in the breeze and whose leaves rustled like paper bags. *But in the end she was just like all the others.*

Nicky fanned the photographs out on the duvet like a pack of cards. He'd taken some pictures of the local area, the shopping centre, the library, the market and the park. But often, when he was walking along, he found himself drawn towards the area where Lesley had lived and most of his photos had been taken there: her street, her front garden, the cars parked along the kerb. He'd even become interested in the derelict house opposite and taken it at a number of angles. In some of the pictures there was a blurry girl, about five foot three, slim with dark curly hair. In one she was wearing a black school uniform, in others she was in jeans and T-shirt; in a couple she was wearing a short skirt and trainers. He

27

was mostly too far away from her to get a clear image.

Except for one picture. He'd been in the front garden of the derelict house, behind an overgrown bush, as she'd been walking along the street. Her hair was pulled up on top of her head, spraying out at the back like a fountain. Her skin was very pale and her head down, her eyes on the pavement. Just as he snapped the picture she'd turned towards him, reaching up to tug at her ponytail. He'd been worried that she might notice him but she'd seemed distracted and turned away again. It was the best shot he had of her and he liked to look at it a lot.

Sending the letter to her had been an impulse act. In the days after the funeral he had been aggravated and jumpy. Pacing up and down his tiny room he'd felt like a cat in a cage. *Powerless*. Lesley's words had shown him that. They were marks on a piece of paper but it was as though she'd spoken to him and he'd not been able to answer. So he wrote his answer on to his own bit of paper and scoured the shops looking for a blue envelope.

Nicky wondered how she had felt when the letter unfolded in her hand. Had the words scalded her? Had her jaw hardened? Had her eyes screwed up into slits? Nicky knew what it felt like to read bad news.

Her name was *Chloe*. He'd known that for a long time. Lesley had talked about her; her daughter who was the same age as Nicky. Before Lesley's letter Nicky had fantasized about this girl whom he had never seen. He had conversations with her in his head. They were like girlfriend and boyfriend. This made him laugh. How silly. What would Lesley Cozens have thought of that?

Now when he thought of Lesley's daughter he felt anger building up inside him. He tossed the photograph aside and lay on the bed, his back stiff, his neck tight. He felt like he wanted to get hold of something and squeeze it until it broke. He turned over, pushed his face into the pillow and forced himself to calm down. After a few moments he felt his shoulders soften. Then there was a tentative knock at the door. Nicky sat up. He shoved the photos under his pillow. Another knock sounded. He wondered if it was Vince, the kid from two doors down. No doubt he'd have his UFO magazine with him full of eye-witness accounts about alien landings on earth. He stood up and stretched his arms and shook his legs, feeling the tension ebb away.

'You in there, Nick? It's me, Trevor.'

If it wasn't one sort of alien it was another.

'Only, I wondered if you fancied coming up the shops with me? We could look at the decks, maybe.'

Nicky tutted. He wished he hadn't told Trevor that he was interested in music production. It had slipped out when he wasn't thinking. Now Trevor was brimming with information about the DJs, IT links, sound equipment, Music Technology college courses. It was like planting a tiny seed and watching a beanstalk grow.

'I'm just coming,' he called out, pulling the photo

of Chloe out from under the pillow and putting it in his back pocket.

If only Trevor would just go back home to his own planet. That would suit Nicky nicely. Wearing a half-smile at his own joke, he opened the door and went out of his room.

6

At Lowestoft, Chloe's grandmother was on the platform
to meet her. Her blonde hair stood out with a pinkish
sheen and she raised an arm to wave enthusiastically.
Chloe gripped tightly on to her bag, not really sure how
she was going to get on.

'Just go for a week.'

Her dad had said it while he was looking at some
architect's plans which he'd laid out on the coffee table in
the living room. He was on the brink of returning to
work, he'd told her, *just to get my mind off things*.

'It'll be good for your gran. And you too.'

She'd nodded and watched him making notes down the
side of the diagram. His lips were moving silently and he
looked like he was doing sums in his head. She'd agreed
to go to please him. A week with a grandmother whom
she hardly knew.

It wasn't as if she had much else to do. A few days
before she'd tried going back to school but it hadn't
lasted. Girls like Lucy or Jo or Terri, all of whom she had
known for years, had smiled and made an immediate
fuss of her when she turned up in class. She'd been

grateful, warmed to them, enjoyed their company.

But it was awkward. Once they got over asking her how she was, how her dad was, they'd inevitably talk about other things. It was a relief at first to hear them discuss the previous night's TV, the latest fashions, the gossip about boys; even serious subjects like plans for college or the exams the following year. There came a point, though, where the words just became noises and Chloe found herself slipping away from them. She shrank back and hid in the shadows of the conversation, their voices at a distance, talking passionately about a new shade of lipstick or a new shopping centre opening. What did it matter, she wanted to whisper. What did any of it matter when her mother had been snatched away from her? The second morning, sitting in the middle of her friends, she looked over at the door of the classroom and thought she saw her mum's face peeping into the room. Then she was gone, leaving just an empty space.

It was better to stay at home. The school understood. By September she would be all right again. There were days, though, when Chloe doubted that she'd ever be right again. She'd lost her direction and the photos sat in piles collecting dust. The blue envelope was there among them curled up at the corners, its contents a little niggle at the back of her mind.

'A disaffected client,' her dad had said dismissively. 'Over the years your mum dealt with loads of children. Most are grown up now. Maybe it's someone who's in a boring job or who's made a bad marriage and they're looking for someone to blame. The fact that Mum died . . . isn't here any more . . . That means they can blame her and she can't answer back.'

Her dad was probably right. It made her feel unhappy, though, whenever she thought of the hard words: *I'm not sorry your mum's dead*. It was another reason to get away from home.

On the station platform her gran walked towards her smiling widely. She stopped a few metres away, inhaled on a cigarette and promptly dropped it, treading it into the ground with a high-heeled shoe.

'Hello, petal,' she said, loudly, reaching her and kissing her on the cheek. 'It's lovely to see you.'

Chloe kissed her gran's powdered cheek.

'I'm definitely giving the fags up,' her gran said, breathing heavily. 'Lesley would *not* approve,' she added, pulling Chloe's hold-all off her and lugging it back up the platform towards the station exit.

At her gran's house she was almost knocked over by the dogs. Two identical Yorkshire terriers bounced up in the air as she went through the front door, barking wildly and nipping gently at her fingers and arms as she squatted down to say hello to them.

'Meet Prince and Queenie,' her gran said, smiling and clucking at the two dogs.

'I didn't know you had these,' Chloe said, squatting down and using both hands to pat the excited animals.

'About six months now. Sonia and me went to pick them up. I only wanted one but that would have meant the other one was left alone. Two for the price of one, the man said, just like a supermarket special offer. This is Prince and that's Queenie. No wait . . .'

The two dogs climbed over each other to be petted. Chloe managed to stand up. She was about to ask who Sonia was when her gran explained.

'You remember Sonia? My neighbour's daughter. She was usually somewhere around when you and your mum came to visit.'

Her gran walked ahead through the living room and into the kitchen and Chloe went up to the spare room. Prince and Queenie followed her, jumping into the air to nibble at her hands or bag. Chloe dumped her bag on the floor and sat on the bed. She heard her gran moving about in the kitchen below, the sound of dishes and cutlery clinking. The dogs shot out of the room and down the stairs. Chloe heard her gran give a shriek of delight at their arrival in the kitchen.

The room was strangely quiet without them.

It was odd that she had never before stayed overnight in her gran's house. But then her mum and her gran had never been that close. There'd even been a long time when they hadn't spoken at all, when she'd been very young. *Five lost years*, her gran had said, at the funeral. They hadn't spoken or seen each other for five years.

After that they'd visited, she and her mum mostly, a

couple of times a year; but they'd only ever come for the day. It meant getting up about six, a two-hour drive and then a day at the seaside. Chloe didn't remember the visits as being enjoyable. Her mum and her gran always started off friendly and affectionate but as the day wore on they began to snipe at each other. Sometimes her gran came to London. She stayed in their spare room and her mum took her out for days to see the sights or shopping. It had always been a bother, never a relaxed time. Gran always had to be catered for; she could never just sit around the house and chat.

In the next-door garden were two people sitting in deckchairs. An old lady in a giant dressing-gown and another woman, much younger; probably Sonia. The younger woman looked up at her and seemed to catch her eye.

A few moments later she was unpacking her bag, putting her jeans and tops in a drawer of the bedside chest. She heard the patter of feet on the stairs and looked up to see Prince and Queenie running into the room ahead of her gran. She had changed out of her high-heeled shoes and into a pair of pink fluffy slippers.

'That's Vera, I don't know if you remember her? Sonia's mum?' her gran said, pulling the net curtain back in place. 'Poor woman's been ill for years. Sonia looks after her.'

Chloe sat down on the bed and her gran sat next to her and put an arm around her shoulder. She felt awkward but her gran didn't seem to notice and leant her head on Chloe's shoulder. Prince and Queenie leapt up and sat overlapping each other on her gran's lap, their tiny pink tongues hanging out. After a minute and what sounded like some sniffing her gran sat up straight, her face pink and her eyes glittering.

'Me and your mum, we weren't as close as we could have been. I'm just glad you're here and we can finally get to know each other.'

Chloe nodded uncertainly and her gran stood up, letting the dogs tumble off her lap.

They did get to know each other. They shopped, they took the dogs to the park, they strolled along the seafront and in and out of the arcades and visited the funfair – her gran pointing out places where her mum used to eat or spend time with her friends. At an ice-cream parlour called Benjy's they stopped and bought some cones.

'Your mum worked here during the summer holidays before she went off to university. Whenever I walked past she always spun me off a free ice cream. Those were the days!'

Her gran winked at her and looked longingly at the shop, a great sigh wheezing out of her. When they were tired they went back to the house and were greeted by Prince and Queenie and more often than not they were joined by Sonia who just appeared at the kitchen back door. She brought treats for the dogs or cream cakes in a cardboard box for her gran. She didn't *visit* exactly, just called by and sat down spending a few minutes or a few hours. Her gran would ask Sonia about how Vera was. *Oh you know, OK,* Sonia would say.

The day before she was due to go back to London they looked at some of her mum's childhood belongings and old photographs. Her gran gave her a couple of pictures to keep.

'These were taken in the spring before you came along. This one's at the seafront. Your mum was heavily pregnant.'

'I didn't know my mum stayed here then,' Chloe said.

'For a week. Your dad was away on a job and your mum didn't want to be on her own. It was just after Easter, quite warm for the time of year. We went all over the place. We had beach walks and even a barbecue. No alcohol, mind. Your mum knew how to take care of herself.'

Chloe picked up the other photograph, which was taken in her gran's back garden. Her mum and her gran and another woman were sitting on deck chairs. Behind the group, standing, was a teenager.

'Is this Sonia?'

'Yes, and that's Vera, when she was well. It was taken by Tom, Vera's husband. He'd just come off a three-month tour of duty in Northern Ireland. Your mum didn't always see eye to eye with Tom but that was a nice night. We had a barbecue and candles in jam jars all over the garden so that when it got dark it was like a fairy palace. That was your mum's idea.'

Chloe looked closer. She could see her mum sitting awkwardly, her hands resting on the bump. Sonia, as a teenager, was leaning on her mum's deck chair.

'Sonia looks so different,' she said, trying to link up the girl in the photo with the older woman from next door.

'She was a sweet girl. Still is. She had a kind of crush on your mum. Hung around her all the time. Lesley didn't mind. The family were a bit stiff, if you know what I mean.'

Chloe suddenly liked Sonia a lot more. She had a crush on Lesley. That didn't surprise her. Who could have failed to like her mum?

A day later she was back home and laid the two new photos on top of the others in her room. Her dad came in while she was unpacking.

'You look tanned,' he said.

'It wasn't exactly hot weather!'

'Well, you look better than you did when you went,' he said.

After he left she looked in the mirror. She did look better. Her hair, which she usually pulled back off her face, was hanging loose. Her skin, which had looked like clotted cream, now had a rosy glow to it. Even her eyes looked brighter. The week away had been good. And her gran hadn't been so bad after all. She gave herself a smile then felt a dull ache in her ribs. Her shoulders fell and she turned away from the mirror. It had only been six weeks or so since the funeral. How could she even *think* like this?

'Some letters for you down here,' her dad shouted up the stairs.

She found three letters on the hall table and frowned as she saw that one of them was in a blue envelope. Leaving the other two aside she looked at the handwriting. Printed letters, neat and formal: *Miss Chloe Cozens*. It felt thin and for a moment she thought of not opening it, just chucking it in the bin. She looked at the other letters and considered opening them first. One had her school stamp on it and the other looked like junk mail. She turned away, though, and put her thumb into the corner of the blue envelope and tore it open.

It wasn't a letter this time. It was a photograph. Her mum in a blouse and skirt, standing by a garden wall. Half of it had been cut off, as if there was another person beside her. Across her mum's face was an angry cross. An X made with a thick felt-tip.

'Do you know I think that trip did you a lot of good.' Her dad's voice came down the hallway before him. 'And me, if I'm honest. Getting back to work was the right thing to do.'

Chloe's jaw clenched at the photo. It was just someone with an old grudge. She held it flat against her chest. She was not going to let it get her down.

'What's that, love?' her dad said.

For the first time she noticed how much better he looked. He'd had his hair cut and was wearing a T-shirt that was ironed and he had a sort of *busy* look about him as if he had things to do.

'Nothing,' she said, folding the photo in half and shoving it back into the envelope. 'Just some junk mail.'

7

It hadn't taken Nicky any time at all to find a way into the derelict building across the road from Lesley Cozens's house. It hadn't been lived in for many years and it didn't seem as though anyone had set foot in it for a very long while. When he'd first decided to go in, a couple of days before, he'd tried pushing against the faded front door. But even though it looked battered, it had stayed firmly shut as though there was a padlock on the other side. He had to find another way in. There was an alley that ran down the back of all the houses and a couple of days later Nicky simply forced the gate open, squashing foot-high grass and sending cobwebs and dust swirling about in a back garden that had the look of a tropical jungle.

He closed the gate carefully so that no one knew he was there. Then he trod gingerly through the overgrown bushes and grass that had taken the garden over. He stopped midway and looked around. The brickwork was crumbling and the windows were covered with splintered wood. The whole structure was grey and had a dead look to it. In contrast the garden seemed alive, the grass and foliage trembling with movement and glistening with moisture.

The back door was easy to open and Nicky went in and explored the old house. He'd been right about the padlock on the front door. The downstairs rooms had been vandalized but those upstairs had been left alone. This was because each of the room doors was locked. Nicky took out his Swiss Army knife and unscrewed one of the locks and let himself into the front bedroom. It was dark even though it was still daylight. After some fiddling he loosened one of the planks of wood that covered the glass. The room was shot through with light and Nicky looked around. It was a large room with a bay window. The walls had been painted white once and the floor was just boards. It looked clean and peaceful and he suddenly felt comfortable there. When he squatted down to look out of the window there was a perfect view of Lesley Cozens's house. He felt pleased with himself. It was as if he was meant to be there, although he didn't exactly know why. Keeping watch, he supposed. Waiting for Chloe Cozens to come out.

He started to go regularly. The exams were finished and the long summer evenings meant that he could stay until it got too dark to see, then he could slip out and go back to Crystal House. When Trevor or anyone asked him what he'd been doing he gave a mysterious shrug. They didn't push him. One night Trevor even said, *Your secret's safe with me, mate.* Trevor was convinced that he had a girlfriend.

A couple of days before, he'd brought some things with him: a blanket from the Crystal House store cupboard and a couple of cushions from the common room that no one would miss. It meant he could relax and sit comfortably.

It had been a slow week though. Nicky had been in his watching place three times. Each time he'd stayed almost four hours but he hadn't seen Chloe at all. That night he bought a sandwich from the baker's and some crisps and a drink. Plus he brought a couple of magazines and a torch in case there wasn't enough light to read by.

He wondered if she'd been too upset to come out. He'd expected to see more of her now that she'd returned from wherever it was that she'd been. He saw her dad a lot, going back and forth from the side entrance of the house to his van, loading and unloading stuff. He imagined her inside the house, sitting by herself, perhaps looking at the picture that he'd sent. In the middle of all his rage he felt an ache of sympathy; as if it wasn't him who had sent the picture or the letter at all but some other person. Then he pulled himself together. It didn't take much for him to remember the blue envelope which held Lesley's letter. A few pieces of paper that had dropped into his life like a slab of stone. He had to be hard. He *deserved* to be hard.

This emotion carried him back to Crystal House at the end of the evening. He walked into the wide hallway with a sense of purpose. Some of the other kids were hanging round but he ignored them. When he went past the front living room Trevor came out and gave him a smile. He put his thumb up as though he knew exactly what Nicky had been doing. Nicky gave him a quick nod. Poor Trevor. He thought he knew everything that was going on.

Not like Lesley Cozens. She wouldn't have been taken in by him. She would have made him tell her what he'd been doing. *You've got to be honest with me*, she'd said, *and I'll always try to do the same with you.*

He had tried his best to be honest with her.

There were times, though, when he wished she hadn't been quite so honest with him.

8

After the week in Lowestoft, Chloe decided to sleep in the back dining room. Her dad carried the futon down from the spare room, moving the furniture round so that it fitted around the low bed.

'I just don't know why you want to sleep in here, love,' her dad said.

She didn't quite know herself. She couldn't explain. When her dad went out she lowered herself on to the bed and sat cross-legged. She held her breath as she looked around the room. Once it had just been a dining room that they hardly ever used: now it was a place that was heavy with memory. Her eye rested on the Welsh dresser with its neat lines of china cups and saucers. Her mum had collected them all. Some were from charity shops and antique fairs; a couple her dad had rescued from houses where he'd done building work. Many had cracks or chips but her mum hadn't cared. *Just because something is damaged that doesn't mean it's no longer beautiful,* she'd said. Chloe felt her throat closing up and she swallowed three or four times.

Her dad popped his head in later.

'It'll only be until I go back to school. Then everything will get back to normal,' she said.

Her dad shrugged his shoulders with incomprehension.

'Whatever you say, love. Oh, and don't forget Mum's stuff at Crystal House. I said you'd go this morning, about tennish? Ask for Trevor Williams. He's the one who rang.'

He went off to work with his shoulders rounded. She watched through the living-room window as he opened the van door. He fiddled with the belt of his jeans and then spent a moment tucking his T-shirt in. All the time he was looking round at the house. She hoped he wasn't going to come back in. When he opened the back of the van and peered in she felt a twinge of guilt. Why should she mind if he came back in? He was her dad. They were both in the same situation, grieving for her mum.

But it wasn't as simple as that. He had thrown himself back into his job. He seemed to be busy every moment of every day. He hardly had the time to have his dinner. He was either on the phone to clients or out in the garage sorting out his tools or doing small pieces of woodwork. In the evenings he often drove out to look at new jobs; houses where married couples wanted two rooms knocked into one or a new conservatory or kitchen extension.

Since she'd returned from her gran's and found the spoilt photo she'd wanted to talk to him about her mum. She wanted to hear him telling her all the good things that her mum had done. How she'd been a brilliant social worker and had helped a lot of damaged people with their lives. But whenever she touched on the subject he always looked away from her and started to pat his trouser pockets as though he was searching for something. Or he mentioned some job he had to do in the garden or in his van.

The days when he cried or got upset in front of her had passed. He closed his bedroom door tightly every night and Chloe sometimes paused outside to see if she could hear anything but there was only silence.

One morning, after he'd gone to work, she went in there to pick up the laundry. She straightened her dad's duvet and puffed his pillows up. Underneath she found a silk nightie that had been her mum's. It was a deep orange colour and had been bought, Chloe remembered, for a holiday in Greece. Seeing it there gave her a momentary shock. She sat on the bed and held it in her hands, feeling the slipperiness of the fabric on her fingers. She knew if she lifted it up to her face there might be the hint of her mother's scent; her perfume or deodorant, her soap or hair shampoo.

She folded it up and placed it back under the pillow. The sight of it there made her feel better somehow. Even though he wasn't talking about her mum any more she was still uppermost in his mind.

He couldn't go and pick her mum's stuff up from her workplace though.

That was exactly why she hadn't shown him the photo.

He was getting on with things and she didn't want to pull him back, make him miserable. Like that day of the funeral when he'd been in charge of everything and then arrived back at the house and seen the broken window. She didn't want to see her dad like that ever again.

She frowned. A photo, a broken window and a letter. These were things she was going to keep to herself.

9

Nicky was listening to Trevor, who was talking about university courses. In his hand he had a thin gold chain with a tiny cross. It was old and he'd owned it for a long time even though he'd never had it round his neck. Trevor was describing a course he'd read about: Computer Studies and Engineering.

'Let's face it, Nick, you've got the ability.'

This was true. Since he'd left the Marshalls' Nicky had had no trouble in school. He kept himself to himself and did the work he was supposed to do. He smiled at the teachers and handed in the homework. Comments like *excellent* and *a very thoughtful piece* littered his work. His teachers had been wary at first; no doubt they had been informed of his reputation in advance. But Nicky had no intention of being violent in school, no plans to hurt anyone. All he asked was that people left him alone.

'Maybe Oxford or Cambridge. Why not?'

They were sitting either side of the table in one of the two kitchens in Crystal House. He had a mug of tea in front of him. Next to it was his mobile. While Trevor was talking he put the chain and cross on the table, shaping it out into a circle with the cross at the bottom.

'What's that, Nick?' Trevor said, with a smile.

Trevor had taken to calling him *Nick*. It was an attempt to be matey and Nicky put up with it with as much politeness as he could. Possibly it was part of his social worker's training. Session Forty-Two: How to be Friends with a Difficult Teenager.

Lesley Cozens had never done this. From the very first she'd seemed so natural with him; as if they were just friends. She hadn't been sugary with him though, she'd tried to be straight. *Pull yourself together*, she'd said, if he'd been moody or surly. When she took him to the Marshalls' she'd laid it on the line.

'Nicky, you're almost at the age where the local authority ceases to have responsibility for you. You need a home and some adults to look out for you. I'm not telling you it'll be happy families and that you'll have a substitute mum and dad. But what's wrong with living somewhere nice with people who care what exams you get and will help you go to college and uni?'

Nicky had smiled. Lesley always called it *uni*. Not university.

'What's the alternative? To live in some place like this until they find a bedsit for you. You don't want that.'

He hadn't wanted that and he'd been keen and enthusiastic going to the Marshalls'. They'd been his last chance. A little island in the middle of a vast ocean. He wanted to make it work. But he hadn't bargained for Ben.

'This is really nice, Nick.'

Trevor had the chain and cross. He must have picked it up off the table, although Nicky had no memory of him reaching across and lifting it away.

'It's a bit lightweight for a bloke. More for a girl. What is it? A present for a girlfriend?'

'*No,*' Nicky said.

Of course. Trevor didn't know anything about him. His case notes had been lost before he even went to the Marshalls'. Would Trevor have bothered to read them anyway?

'Actually, Trevor, I've got some stuff to do,' Nicky said, standing up, holding his hand out for the cross and chain.

'Right you are. Maybe see you later? No, wait. I've got a meeting on this afternoon. Maybe in the morning?'

Nicky gave a vague nod that didn't mean yes or no, picked up his mobile, and walked off towards the stairs and his room. As he opened his door, Vince, the kid from along the corridor, appeared out of nowhere. He was holding his usual UFO magazine, pretending to read it. He looked up and walked towards Nicky.

'All right, Nicky?' he said, leaning one shoulder against the wall.

Nicky nodded and left the door open so that Vince could follow him into his room. He sat sideways across his bed with his hands in his jeans and looked at the magazine which Vince was carrying. He could see the headline:

Alien Invasion of Seaside Town.

'They've got evidence,' Vince said, rapidly, 'photographs, and footprints.'

'Oh yeah?' Nicky said with a half-smile.

'I know you don't believe it but . . .'

Vince looked round and pulled Nicky's desk chair out. He unzipped his jacket and made himself comfortable.

'You could take the jacket off,' Nicky said, settling himself back on the bed. Vince always wore his jacket, no matter what the weather. Some of the other kids swore that he slept in it.

'No, I'm all right.'

Vince opened the magazine and Nicky heard the words *Roswell incident*. He knew he was in for a long explanation. He let the boy talk. Why not? As long as he nodded his head from time to time, where was the harm?

'At Roswell, they actually found one of the creatures. It was all hushed up by the American secret service but someone filmed the alien. It was on telly, I saw it with my own eyes.'

'Yeah,' Nicky said.

'What's this?'

Vince was holding up a half of a photograph that had been lying on the desk top. Nicky looked at it with some consternation. It showed him leaning against a brick wall. It had been taken in front of the Marshalls' house.

'What happened to the rest?'

Nicky shrugged and Vince went back to looking at his magazine.

'Anyway,' Vince said, finally. 'What you up to? Fancy having a look round the shopping centre?'

'No, I can't, I've got somewhere to go.'

Nicky stood up and Vince fiddled with his jacket, zipping it up again with vigour.

'See you later,' he said, closing the room door behind him.

Nicky looked at the photograph and tried to push down a feeling of remorse. He closed his eyes. Why should he feel bad about the things he did? He felt his hand stiffen with irritation. He was the victim here, not Lesley's stupid daughter. He had to be careful of softening. His old social worker had been dead for two months. Her family still had their memories. What did he have? Nothing. He tossed the photo to the side and stood up flexing his fingers, trying to flush the tension out. Then he went across to his drawer and found the tiny black box he had where he kept the cross and chain. He lay it down and packed it away. He put his jacket on and went out.

10

Crystal House was smaller than she'd expected it to be. It was on the bend of a road, a high hedge edging the narrow garden. It was a long building with two storeys. On either side of it were regular houses and some shops. Some of the upstairs windows were open and there was music floating out. Chloe had expected something quite different. A huge brick building in the middle of its own grounds. The word *orphanage* jumped into her head. It was old-fashioned and not used but still she couldn't help but think of some kind of Victorian institution with bedraggled children and cruel matrons. In all the years that her mum had worked there she'd never visited. Not once. Her mum had said that it was because it was a place that was home to the children and they had rights. They didn't want the staff's relatives plodding through, sightseeing.

Chloe walked the length of the building to find the entrance. The main door had a bell beside an intercom. She pressed the button and waited. A man opened the door.

'Yes?'

He was mid-twenties. He had jeans on and a short-sleeved shirt with a loosely knotted tie. His hair was cropped and he wore small penny glasses that made his eyes look perfectly round. Around his neck was an identity tag.

'I'm Chloe,' she said. 'Lesley Cozens's daughter?'

She was distracted by a couple of girls walking down the hall behind him. One of them gave her a stare.

'Chloe! Nice to see you. Come in. I've got all Mrs Cozens's stuff ready. I'm Trevor, by the way. I didn't know your mum, but I know that everyone here misses her a lot.'

She followed him along a dark hallway into an office. There were two desks with computers. Around each were piles of papers and folders.

'I put her stuff here,' he said, bending over.

He pointed to a large box. It was a box that had been used to carry wine. Her mum's name was written neatly on the outside in thick black pen and she could see the edge of her mum's purple scarf peeping over the top. Her throat tightened up. She'd completely forgotten about that scarf.

'Cup of tea?' Trevor said, stroking his tie. 'Sugar? Milk?'

She nodded. Why not? It was quite nice, being there, in that room where her mum had spent so many hours. When Trevor left she sat in a soft chair that had its back against the wall. She pulled the box towards her and was about to sort through when the door swung open and a boy walked in and headed straight for one of the desks where a pile of magazines sat.

'All right if I take this?' he said to no one in particular.

He glanced up in Chloe's direction and then away. A second later, he looked back, his face puzzled.

'I'm picking something up,' Chloe said, feeling the need to explain. 'My mum used to work here.'

He didn't say a word, just looked at her. Trevor arrived with a mug of tea.

'Hi, Nick!' he said, cheerfully. 'Here you are, Chloe.'

'My name's *Nicky*,' the lad said tersely, looking sideways at Chloe.

'Sorry, mate. Hey, do you want a drink? Kettle's just boiled.'

Nicky shook his head and then looked down at the magazine. He seemed annoyed about something. Chloe could feel the tension coming off him like cold air.

Trevor turned to her. 'Chloe, this was your mum's desk. I use it now.' Then he turned back to Nicky. 'That's when I get a chance to sit down, right, Nick? There's always so much to do here but then I don't need to tell you that. You know how hard social workers work. Sure you don't want a drink, Nick?'

Nicky shook his head and moved closer to the door as if he was going to walk out. The front door bell rang and Trevor tutted and went towards it, pulling the office door closed behind him. Chloe sipped her tea. Nicky looked up from his magazine and caught her eye. She gave a tiny smile, not sure if he was friendly or not. He closed his magazine and stared at her. Chloe coughed into her hand. She felt uncomfortable. It wasn't right for her to be there. It was this boy's home and she was just picking stuff up.

'I have to go in a minute,' Chloe said, taking a gulp of hot tea, trying to drink it as quickly as possible.

'I knew your mum. She was my social worker. I'm Nicky Nelson . . .' he said, sounding awkward.

Chloe nodded. She waited in case he had anything else to say. He was tall and thin and was wearing dark-coloured jeans that looked new. He had a short-sleeved T-shirt on and Chloe found herself focusing on a set of red scars across his forearm. When she looked up he was staring at her, his dark spiky hair making his skin look pale and ghostly. He smiled suddenly, pointing at the scarf she was holding.

'Your mum was always wearing that. That and her leather jacket.'

Chloe felt her spirits rise. She pulled at the scarf, letting it billow out of the box.

'I know. She *loved* her leather jacket. My dad bought it for her.'

'What about the scarf?' he said.

'I bought it . . .'

All of a sudden she was in tears. She blinked and wiped them away with the edge of the scarf but they kept coming. Nicky leant back on the desk looking embarrassed. Chloe gave a couple of loud sniffs and stood up, placing her half-finished tea on the desk.

'Sorry . . . I just . . . do this now and then. It's only been a few weeks . . .' She bent down to pick up the box.

The door opened and Trevor stood there.

'Everything all right?' he said, looking at each of them.

'I must go,' she said, sliding her hands under the box.

'I'd give you a lift but I'm on call. Have you got far to go?'

'No, really. I can manage,' she said, holding the underside of the box as if it was a tray.

'Go on, Nick, open the door for the girl!' Trevor said.

'I'm fine,' she said. She began to walk along the hallway but had to stop at the front door.

She heard footsteps and Nicky was there reaching across her, opening the front door. She thanked him and walked along the path past a group of younger boys draped over the front gate. A couple of them spoke to Nicky and she realized that he was still behind her.

'Let me help. I'm going your way,' he said, taking the box from her, managing a half-smile.

He didn't say much. When they got on the bus he headed for the back seat. He sat by the window with the box beside him. Chloe sat on the other side. On top of the box sat the purple scarf. Underneath, it looked like there were personal things; a couple of cups, tea bags, photos. Almost forgetting that Nicky was there, she began to rummage through and after a moment she pulled out a pencil-case. It was black leather and she'd bought it for her mum as a Christmas present a number of years before. It looked battered and felt thin in places. She looked up and caught Nicky staring at her.

'I bought this . . .' she started.

He nodded. He picked up the scarf and felt the fabric. Then he unravelled it. She unzipped the pencil-case and looked inside. A couple of pens and a bunch of highlighters. Her mum's favourite.

'How long did you know my mum?'

'Eighteen months,' he said. 'She organized a placement for me. A new family. That's how we got to know each other.'

'But you still saw her?'

'She visited. Every few weeks. And she rang me on my mobile. She was always giving me a quick call. Or texting me,' Nicky said, turning the scarf over and over in his hands.

Chloe nodded. 'Me too,' she smiled. 'Right in the middle of a lesson she'd send me a text about popping into the supermarket or telling me she'd be late. She was always late for everything.'

'You're right, she was! She often said, *I'll be round about five or six*, but she never was.'

Chloe put the pencil-case back and pulled out a tube of hand cream.

'I always knew she wouldn't be on time for an

appointment,' Nicky said leaning back in his seat, the purple scarf still in his hands.

'She didn't like watches,' Chloe said, as if that explained it.

'She was too busy. She always had too much to do. Not like Trevor.'

'Oh?'

'Her replacement. Sits on his backside a lot of the time.'

They were coming near to her stop.

'Thanks for helping me,' she said.

'It's nothing. It's not like I had anything else to do,' he said, shrugging it off.

He didn't speak again and she felt his mood had changed. When the bus stopped they got off.

'It's just down here,' she said.

Nicky was walking slightly ahead of her, holding the box, his shoulders rounded. He was silent and she found herself talking on about this and that just to cover up the silence. At her house she got her keys out.

'D'you want to come in?' she said, pushing the front door open and taking the box from him. Her arms brushed against his as he handed it to her. She could smell something from him. Spearmint.

He shook his head.

'Thanks for coming. It was really nice of you.'

He had a nice face, even though it seemed to be in a constant frown. He was young but well built, the sort of lad that girls in school might look at a second time.

'See you,' he said, backing down her path. He turned at the last minute and went out of the gate. She watched for a minute, her hand ready to wave if he turned round.

He didn't. So she went inside carrying her mum's box with her.

Getting on the bus back to Crystal House Nicky headed for the back seat and sat down. He felt something in his pocket and pulled out the purple scarf and tutted. He must have put it there when he was on the bus or walking down the street.

He had been preoccupied talking to Chloe Cozens.

He remembered looking at her when she'd been sorting through her mum's things. Her hair had looked as though it had just been washed and hadn't quite dried; shiny, flyaway, wisps of it floating around her face. She had a jacket on but underneath was a bright blue V-neck T-shirt. He'd looked at her neck and her chest, her skin creamy and soft, and for a moment he'd wanted to reach over and touch her. *Pathetic, Stupid*. This girl, this sad-eyed girl, was not going to have an effect on him.

Back in Crystal House he found Peter Robinson, a tall thin lad with a broken-heart tattoo on his neck, blocking up the hallway. Nicky stood back for a moment reluctant to say anything, hoping that the pale-faced kid would move of his own accord.

Nicky had learnt how to get by in local council homes.

At first he'd tried to act big. But it never worked. There was always some other kid who was tougher and nastier. It didn't matter that he'd had a hard life. The other kids had no sympathy for him because they had experienced similar stuff themselves. More than likely they couldn't stand the sight of him because he reminded them of their own sorry situation. As soon as he arrived at some new house the toughest kid usually made themselves known. *Watch it, I'm in charge*, they seemed to say. These boys walked around the place like royalty. Peter Robinson was that kind of kid. He always had loads of money and could be seen hanging round the precinct waiting for older boys or men to buy him alcohol. Sometimes he smoked dope out in the back garden. Nicky had watched him through his bedroom window sitting in the middle of three or four kids, the light on the end of one cigarette passed from person to person.

Nicky avoided him. That night he was stuck in the hall waiting for him to move on. A couple of other boys were with him and Nicky couldn't see what they were all focusing on. A girl was leaning over the banister.

'Oh Pete, leave him alone, he's only a kid.'

'Get lost. He shouldn't have been in my room.'

Nicky heard a whimpering sound from the corner.

Peter Robinson laughed and Nicky saw his foot rise and kick the wall. A gap opened and he could see Vince being held in a loose headlock by one of Peter Robinson's mates. Vince was using one hand to try and pull the older boy's arm away. With the other he was trying to shield his groin from the threat of Peter Robinson's foot. His face, above his zipped-up jacket, was red and tearful.

'I never touched nothing!'

'You shouldn't have been there at all!'

'What's going on?' Nicky said.

Vince was nosey, that was his problem. Where Nicky kept himself to himself, Vince was always hanging round, trying to be a part of other people's lives.

'I never knew it was Pete's room,' Vince lied.

Peter Robinson reached across and grabbed the younger boy's earlobe and began to twist it.

'Leave the kid alone,' Nicky said.

His voice was calm but inside he felt agitated, his breath short. He wanted nothing more than to go up to his room but he couldn't leave Vince. He was just a stupid kid, that was all. Couldn't Robinson leave him be?

'Let him go.' Nicky spoke again, his voice deliberately light, a forced smile on his face.

Without releasing Vince's ear Peter Robinson turned and swore at Nicky. The other boys smirked and Vince let out a high-pitched squeal.

Where was Trevor? Or any of the other workers? How come they were never around when something like this happened?

'I only went in there for a minute. Suze was chasing me. I just went in there to get out of her way,' Vince said, breathlessly.

'So how come my stuff's all mucked up?'

Peter Robinson's words had a whining sound. He'd let go of Vince's earlobe and was using his finger to prod the middle of Vince's forehead. His mate had dropped the headlock and was leaning back against the wall looking bored. Vince was standing like a statue, the older boy's finger pinning him to the wall. Nicky relaxed. The moment had passed. There wasn't going to be any violence. It was all talk and threat; nasty enough in its own way but maybe Vince had it coming to him. One way and another it would be a good lesson. There were bad people in life and the best thing to do was to avoid them.

'You're not going to go in my room again, are you, Vince, my boy?'

Peter Robinson's voice was like saccharine, sweet and fake. Nicky stepped by to walk towards the stairs. Out through a window he could see Trevor's car pulling up. Too late to be of any use to anyone.

'Otherwise,' he heard Peter Robinson summing up, 'I might have to take your wet sheets out and show them to some of your girlfriends.'

Nicky stopped in his tracks. He felt a stifled giggle ripple along the hallway and turned to see Vince's face. The young boy's expression had transformed. His mouth was twisted up with shame and his eyes were blinking back fresh tears.

'What's up?' Peter Robinson said. 'Don't you like people to know about your night-time problems?'

Nicky retraced his steps and stood behind the knot of boys.

'Peter, leave the kid alone,' he said, an edge to his voice.

'Maybe it's not you! Maybe it's one of them aliens who comes every night and pees in your bed.'

Nicky put his hand on the older boy's shoulder. He could just see the broken-heart tattoo, in purple and pink with a jagged break down the middle like a streak of lightning.

'I told you to pack it in,' he said, his voice deeper.

He looked at Vince. The kid's face had sagged, his mischievous eyes and silly grin were gone and he was using his fist to wipe his nose.

'Oh Vince, man, maybe you should wear a nappy!' Peter Robinson said, half turning to smirk at Nicky.

The other boys laughed enthusiastically and Nicky's arm shot across the older boy's neck and pulled him backwards down on to the floor of the hallway. Peter Robinson hadn't expected it and fell badly, his head hitting the banisters on the way. The laughter gone, Nicky threw his leg over him and squatted on his chest.

'I told you to shut up,' he shouted, his voice like a juggernaut, his hands pinning the lad's shoulders to the floor. All the time he could feel him struggling beneath him. Taller and older he might have been; but he was thin and weak and without his mates he was no match.

From somewhere behind, Nicky heard room doors opening and shutting, the sound of footsteps and voices cascading down the stairs. The buzz of excitement that comes with a fight. There was also the familiar sound of Trevor's voice. *Nick, don't do anything silly…*

Peter Robinson tried to raise himself off the floor and began to shout obscenities. The kid was stupid. If he'd just lie still, just stay in one place. Apologize. Did it take so much to say sorry to a tiny hopeless boy like Vince? What was to be gained by showing him up, by telling everyone what his problems were? Who cared what the sheets were like under a duvet? Who cared?

Peter Robinson's hands were pulling at his arms. Nicky loosened up, sat back, flexing his hands. The older boy lifted his head off the ground and one by one Nicky's fists slammed into his cheek and then the side of his nose. There was a gasp as his head fell back down on to the floor and blood oozed out of his nostril like a glug of tomato ketchup.

'Nicky!'

He could hear Trevor's voice at his ear as he lifted one leg and got off the unconscious boy as though he was a horse that he'd been riding. He shook Trevor's arm off and glanced over at Vince who was being hugged by one of the girls. The boy looked gratefully at him. Nicky turned away. He didn't want thanks. He'd hadn't done it for him. He'd done it for himself.

Upstairs, in his room, with the door tightly shut, Nicky felt his hands and his arms begin to shake. He tried to make them rigid and pushed them flat against his jeans.

He felt something in his pocket. The purple scarf. He pulled it out by its corner, scrunched it up in his hands and threw it down on to the floor.

All he asked was to be left alone.

11

The next day Chloe sorted out the contents of the box that her mum's work stuff had come in. There were no surprises. She lay the things out on the bed in the back dining room. Apart from the things she'd already seen there was a diary and an address book; a framed photograph of Chloe and her dad and one of the three of them all together. There was a packet of herbal tea bags, blackcurrant flavour, and a zip-up bag with deodorant and toothpaste in it, a lipstick and some foundation.

She looked in the diary, holding her breath as she flicked through the pages. The early part of the book, up until the end of March, was full of lists and lines of writing, times, ticks, asterixes, underlining, exclamation and question marks. Each page seemed to be full up with layers of words, all added at different times in various pens. There was colour as well. Her mum had had a system for indicating whether something had been done, an appointment kept or a phone call made. She used a fluorescent highlighter pen over the original words. The pages were covered in swathes of lime green, shocking pink and dazzling yellow. Her mum liked her rainbow-coloured pages. It meant that she'd achieved all the little things she'd set out to do that week.

On March 23rd was the line: *Hospital appointment Dr Reynolds, King Thomas 3.25*. The day when Lesley got her test results.

There were still appointments after that date, half a dozen or so that had been made in advance. But the words sat in the middle of an empty page, the handwriting neat, looking small and unimportant, telling of a meeting or an event that Lesley had intended to go to. Meetings that never took place.

Except for one.

Chloe looked at the first week of April. On the Wednesday morning was a line of writing that had a dash of pink highlighter across it.

Nelson Social Worker (Barbara Dunn): Lowestoft 10.30.

It looked like the only appointment her mum had kept. After that the pages were blank. No dates circled or comments of any kind, each page crisp, white, silent. She'd been too ill to do anything. And yet she had managed to go to Lowestoft and meet with a fellow social worker. It must have been important, Chloe thought. The name *Nelson* was fresh in her mind; Nicky Nelson, the boy who helped her home with the cardboard box the day before, a client of her mum's.

She closed the diary and left it on the edge of her bed. Outside the French doors the bootlace cat was turning in circles, its tail in the air curled at the end.

'Come in,' she whispered.

It stood perfectly still for a second, then darted off out of sight.

She took the tea bags and put them back into the kitchen. Then she took the rest of the stuff upstairs to her room. She put the photographs on her chest of drawers and the make-up and hand cream into her underwear drawer. She stood for a moment looking round her room. On the floor by the window sat the five albums that she'd bought. They held the photographs that she'd sorted out. Altogether they gave the *photographic biography* that her dad had talked about. It had taken a while but she'd enjoyed sorting through the images and putting them into chronological order. Her mum's early life in Lowestoft and the years she spent at university. The wedding came next and the training to be a social worker. A year in a run-down part of London dealing with broken families and troubled people. She'd qualified without any problems. But then her mum was brainy and hardly ever failed at anything. Just as she was about to start her job she had fallen pregnant.

It was a funny phrase to use, *fallen pregnant*. Like stumbling into something unexpected. *You were not planned!* she often said to Chloe. *You were an accident.* Another strange statement, as if having her first baby was like a car crash. *I'll tell you what,* her mum had said another time, *having you was like winning the lottery.*

Only the ten pound prize, her dad had added, jokily.

She had hardly started her job as a social worker when she had to take maternity leave. Just before she gave birth to Chloe she spent a week with her mum at Lowestoft. A week by the seaside, sleeping in her old room. Chloe had added the new photos. Her mum, pregnant, sitting next to Gran in the garden, the next-door neighbours holding their glasses up and smiling at the camera. Everyone looked relaxed and happy, especially her gran and her mum. After that Chloe had been born and her gran and her mum had not seen each other for five years. There'd been a falling-out. That time was full of photos of her mum holding Chloe at various ages: newborn, toddler, tiny child. Then, somehow, Gran started to be in the pictures again. Gran and Lesley and Chloe on a visit to an amusement park. Gran, once again, friends with Mum.

The door bell rang and she replaced the album and went downstairs. The boy from Crystal House, Nicky Nelson, was standing at the door. Twice in two days. It gave her an odd feeling.

'Hi,' he said, holding the purple scarf up. 'I came to return this. I must have shoved it in my pocket by mistake.'

'Oh,' she said, shyly, 'I hadn't even realized . . . It's Nicky, isn't it? Come in for a minute.'

He looked as though he wasn't sure, as though he might back away at any moment.

'Please come in. My dad's out. I'm sick of being on my own.'

'OK.' He shrugged and walked past her into the hall.

'I'll get some drinks. We can sit in the garden.'

Once in the kitchen she became businesslike, talking herself through the task of getting the cold drinks. *Sit down for a mo. Here, orange juice OK? Much nicer with some ice. Big glass? I'm thirsty too. These ice cubes are not really ice. What I mean is they're plastic but they're full of liquid and you freeze them. They don't melt in the glass and you con use them again. There! Why don't we go out into the garden?*

Nicky didn't say a word. He took the glass off her and she thought there might be the beginning of a smile on his lips.

'What did you do to your arm?' she said when they'd sat down, him on a plastic chair and her on a low brick wall.

'I scratched it. Against a wall. I can't really remember.'

'It looks deep,' she said.

'I did scratch it. Honest, here,' he thrust his arm out, 'feel it and see.'

'Sorry,' she said, taking a drink and averting her eyes. She'd been too personal.

'No, I mean it. Feel it.'

She reached out and touched his arm. Under her fingers she could feel the raised skin, the scar tissue. It wasn't a graze. She looked up and her face was close to his.

'Your garden's nice.'

He was looking straight at her, a kind of stare that she

couldn't break. She blinked a few times and moved her fingers off his arm.

'My mum did it . . .' she said. 'She's . . . she *was* the gardener. She was always quarrelling with my dad about his stuff. He's a builder and he uses that corner of the garden to keep his tools in. Trouble is he's always bringing stuff home from jobs. Old fireplaces and things.'

She was talking too much again. She stood up as if to stretch her legs. Nicky sat still, his legs splayed out, hardly moving.

'Are you still at school?' she said.

She had no idea about his age. She had no idea about anything. She remembered then her mum's diary and the note in it about her mum seeing the *Nelson Social Worker*.

'Yes,' he said, 'for the moment.'

'I've just finished the first year of my "A" levels,' she said, as though he'd asked.

'Why don't you sit down?' he said. 'Relax.'

'I'm just nervous. I'm not very good around . . .'

'Your mum's clients?'

'No, no, I wasn't going to say that,' she said, sitting on the wall again, her legs crossed, her arms folded. 'I'm not very good in some social situations.'

She meant that wasn't very good with boys but she wasn't going to say it.

'What did your mum die of?' he said suddenly, the word *die* sounding hard, a discordant note in a conversation that had started to feel easy.

'Breast cancer,' she said. 'She was very young to have it . . . It was aggressive . . .'

She stopped. It wasn't that she was going to cry but a lump had formed in her throat and no amount of swallowing would dislodge it. He seemed to sense it because he leant forward, his elbows on his knees.

'I'm sorry. Lesley was all right to me.'

Chloe nodded. After a few awkward minutes he spoke again.

'You make friends easily,' he said.

'Not usually,' she said, shrugging her shoulders, looking straight at him. It was difficult not to be flirtatious with him. He looked so fresh, so mischievous. She couldn't help but like him.

'Lesley worked with me for a long time,' he said after a moment, the palms of his hands joined and pointing to the floor. 'Did she ever mention me?'

'She didn't talk about any of her clients.' She coughed lightly. 'It was a policy . . .'

'She must have said something now and then about some of us?'

'Not usually,' Chloe said. 'She was very professional.'

'Did she ever get . . . upset? I mean, bad things happened. It must have affected her?'

He wanted her to say that her mum had talked about him. It seemed important and she felt herself warm to him, this lad who had feelings about her mum. She leant towards him, wanting to backtrack and remember something for him. It would be a lie, though, and she didn't want to do that. She reached out her hand and touched his arm, her fingers just brushing against his skin.

'She did get upset and she might talk about something that had happened but she'd never mention any names,' she said, pulling back, feeling foolish.

He nodded and finished the rest of his drink in one go. He turned and looked at the open French doors. 'Why have you got a bed in there?' he said, standing up and walking across.

'I'm sleeping there at the moment,' she said. 'It was where Mum was in those last weeks.'

He nodded some understanding and then stepped inside. She followed him quickly, feeling uneasy.

'It's a real mess,' she said, looking round with surprise to see the bootlace cat curled into a circle on the bed.

He did an about-turn and she almost walked into him. He was only a footstep away.

'You're not what I expected,' he said and put his hands on her arms, pulling her towards him.

Then he kissed her. It was just a peck on the mouth but it sent a spurt of pleasure through her chest and legs. Her eyes were wide open but his were shut. She could smell spearmint from him again and feel the warmth of his chest. Embarrassed, she took a step backwards, away from the kiss. He opened his eyes and looked at her with a half-smile. Mocking her again.

'Don't be nervous!' he said.

'I told you I'm not very good in some situations . . .' she said.

He picked up the diary on the bed and flicked through.

'Is this your mum's?' he said pleasantly, not obviously put out by her withdrawal. 'I remember seeing this loads of times,' he went on. 'She was always checking what she had to do. She carried it everywhere. I said to her, *Your life would fall apart if you didn't have that diary!*'

'I know,' Chloe said. 'Even if she promised to go shopping with me she put it in there. Look, there's something in there you might be interested in.'

She took the diary from him and flicked through to the page in April where her mum had put *Nelson Social Worker (Barbara Dunn): Lowestoft 10.30*. She held it open for him to look at.

'This is one of the last work things my mum did. Some meeting about you.'

He seemed to look at it for a long time. She expected him to speak but he didn't. She kept looking down at the entry and then back up, expecting him to meet her eyes. His head stayed bent though his face was unreadable. Eventually he gave a slow nod.

'Probably about me,' he said, putting the diary down. 'I should go.'

'Really?' she said, disappointed.

'All right if I use the toilet?' he said.

'Course, it's upstairs. Go straight through that door. I'll just get the glasses in.'

She went out into the garden and picked up the empty glasses. She found herself smiling. Nicky's visit had broken what would have been a long empty day. Maybe she could ask him to come again, she thought, remembering the kiss, letting her finger press on her lips for a second. Why not? It wasn't as if she'd gone out to find this boy. In fact it had come about *because* of her mum. That was the link.

She heard a door slam suddenly. The front door. She walked swiftly in through the kitchen and into the hall.

'Nicky?' she called.

Had he left? Without saying goodbye?

'Nicky? Are you upstairs?'

There was no answer and she opened the front door and looked up the street, expecting to see him walking away. There was no one in either direction. Her shoulders drooped with disappointment. What had she said? Had she been over-friendly, overwhelming perhaps?

She just didn't know what to do, how to act. It was a fact. She was just no good with boys.

12

The money lay on Nicky's bed. All three hundred pounds of it. He'd cleared his account out and the man in the building socicty had smiled at him and asked if he was buying himself something nice. An iPod and speakers, Nicky had told him, pleasantly. Another day, another time it might have been the truth. He enjoyed music. He had his own CDs and vinyls. He'd toyed with the idea of buying decks so that he could practise mixing sounds. He'd done a lot of that at the Marshalls', downloading stuff from the internet. It was Ben who had showed him how to do it.

But that was a lifetime ago.

The money was in tens and twenties and Nicky folded each note up individually. Then he picked up a tiny sock that he'd taken from the laundry cupboard and put the notes into it. Standing up, he unzipped his fly and tucked the sock behind the zip so that when he fastened his jeans it sat there and didn't move. It was a way of making sure that the money didn't get stolen. If he was going to leave Crystal House he had to have some solid cash.

Also on the bed were the pages that he had torn from

Lesley Cozens's diary. He looked at them and felt a swirl of emotion. His surname in her diary. That was his only connection to her. He picked up the pages and screwed them up into a ball.

He was leaving Crystal House.

Not because of Peter Robinson. Since his bloody nose the boy with the tattoo didn't have quite such a swagger and his voice didn't carry so loudly through the house. Nor was he going because of Vince. Since the fight he'd hardly been able to step out of his room without tripping over the lad. Did Nicky want him to go to the shop? Did Nicky want to play cards? Was Nicky going to play football? It was as though he needed to know where Nicky was every minute of the day. Nicky felt some sympathy for Vince but he wasn't his dad or his brother. He would have to manage on his own. He wasn't even leaving because of Trevor, although in the last few days the man was certainly getting on his nerves. After the violence he had reminded Nicky that it wasn't the first time he had physically hurt somebody, there was always poor Ben to think about. *Poor Ben Marshall.* Only occasionally did Nicky feel any remorse for Ben. Mostly he felt nothing. All the same he nodded his head and agreed with Trevor about looking into some counselling sessions. If it kept him happy what was wrong with that?

Nicky was leaving because he wanted to live on his own.

He was tired of always having other people around,

caring for him, organizing him, analysing the things he did. He wanted to be free of it. To live in a space where no one knew about him, where there wasn't a file in a drawer or on a computer screen with his life story on it.

The other kids got him down as well, all of them victims of some sort of personal disaster. He had nothing against any of them individually but he didn't want to be billeted with them. It was as though they'd all been survivors of some traffic pile-up and from then on were sentenced to live together under the same roof, seeing each other every day, reminding each other of their own misfortune.

He didn't want it any more. He was getting near the age when he would be moving on anyway. At some point Trevor would start to talk about university or sheltered accommodation. Or he would be considered for a flat or bedsit. Instead of living in a community, he would be gently dropped into the outside world, like a parachutist over enemy territory.

On the floor of his room his rucksack was packed. A lot of his stuff was already at the house in Warwick Lane. He'd bought a cool box to keep some food in and some candles to light the place at night. All that was left to take were his personal things: the gold cross and chain that was in its box; a few clothes and some toiletries. What else did he need? Nothing.

Crystal House was quiet. The bedside clock showed the time. It was 01:23 a.m. He pulled his rucksack towards him. He put his fingers into the front pocket to get his keys out so that he could leave them on the bedside table. He pulled out a wad of stuff, a couple of letters from school, old bus passes, an exam timetable. At the back was the blue envelope. He unfolded it and took out the second envelope, which held the letter from Lesley.

Dear Nicky, it said, *I'm writing because I don't know if I'm going to see you again. I'm very ill but I have something I have to tell you. Something you have a right to know.*

You've not had a happy life, I know. Your placements haven't worked out, especially with the Marshalls.

The thing is, and I don't quite know how to put this, I feel responsible. You are unhappy because of decisions I made, choices I took. If I had done things differently your life may have been better . . .

Nicky stopped looking at the paper. The words played on in his head, like a tape-recording that he couldn't stop. He imagined her voice speaking, softly, with regret. A phrase here, a sentence there, a breathless paragraph. It all added up to the same thing. Lesley Cozens had made decisions that had mucked up his life. And yet he'd told her daughter that he thought she was *all right*. Inside, his emotions were all over the place. What was happening to him?

He looked down and saw the ball of screwed-up paper from Lesley's diary. He picked it up and pulled it apart. *Nelson Social Worker (Barbara Dunn): Lowestoft 10.30.* Of course she would have met Barbara Dunn. How else would she have found the truth?

He felt his insides harden. Sometimes he just wanted to hit out and hurt someone; he had wanted to punish Lesley Cozens but that wasn't possible. She was dead. Only Chloe was left. A few days before, though, he'd kissed her on the mouth. Where had that come from? What had pushed him towards her? He saw her face for a moment. She'd backed off, shy and awkward. He didn't think she'd had much experience with boys or sex. Nicky gave a rueful smile. He'd had experience; enough to last him a lifetime, he thought.

He'd only gone there to see Lesley's house, to be in her rooms, to sit in her chairs. What on earth had drawn him to her daughter? To put his mouth on hers? And then to leave like that; to take the pages from the diary? Sometimes he didn't recognize himself.

Using his fingers, he gently tore the crinkled paper in half and half again. The pieces he shoved back into his rucksack pocket. There was no point in letting himself get upset. That way led to violence; more social workers, more people interfering in his life.

When the house was quiet and still he stood up and picked up his stuff. Opening his room door quietly he crept down the hall. He paused for a moment outside Vince's door. He could hear the sound of the TV very low. The boy was still awake.

He could say goodbye but what would be the point? It wouldn't make him feel any better and it wouldn't help Vince. The kid had to learn to stand on his own two feet.

Nicky walked on, quietly opening and closing the fire door, and out into the dark night.

13

Chloe looked at the two prospectuses that were sitting on the armchair in the back dining room. They both showed pictures of university campuses. Long glass buildings surrounded by green landscape. Her friend Lucy had brought them around the previous day.

She ought to look at them, research the courses, have some plan in mind for when she went back to school in September. It would be time to apply for uni. To choose a place where she would spend three years.

Lucy had stayed for a while and filled her in with all the gossip from the kids she knew at school. They were mostly on holiday, away or relaxing at home, a couple with jobs; just glad that the first year of 'A' levels was over. *Come out with us one night*, Lucy had said and Chloe had nodded.

She knew she wouldn't go.

It made sense, though, to make plans for the future.

I don't mind you taking a gap year but you need to get a place at university first! Her mum had been adamant. There had never been any suggestion that she would do anything other than go to university. Oxford or Cambridge; Durham or Exeter. Why not? She could get the necessary points. She was a hard worker. For years she had guarded her reputation as a high-flier; top grades and teachers' admiration were things she took for granted.

When her mum fell ill none of it mattered. Her plans were like a house of cards that had simply folded in on itself. After the funeral her future seemed flat and empty; a long colourless road ahead of her. She had to make the journey but was weary before she'd even taken a step.

She made herself open a prospectus. She saw the smiling faces of students looking up at her; sitting at computers or holding ring binders; students in the library or wearing earphones in a language lab. They were grinning at the camera, looking pleased with themselves, carefree. They would sit in lectures or seminars; study in the library; socialize in the bar. They might talk about work or student loans or politics or their love lives.

Chloe took a deep breath. Would she ever be carefree like that again? Would she ever wake up in the morning without feeling that heavy ache, that *knowledge* that her lovely, funny, bright Mum was gone?

She closed the prospectus and noticed that the bootlace cat was at her feet. He had come in through the French doors and was twisting and turning through her legs. She squatted down and stroked the top of his head and neck.

She glanced to the side and saw, with surprise, her mum's diary lying on the floor at the edge of the futon. She frowned, reaching across, her movement disturbing the cat who minced off towards the doors. What's that doing there? she thought, standing up, dusting the outside of the book with the tip of her blouse. She let it fall open as she did it and noticed the jagged edges of paper where some pages had been taken.

She knew, in that instant, with certainty, that Nicky Nelson had taken them. The pages had been roughly torn, from the outer corner across the middle to the spine. As if he had grabbed a few together and just pulled.

She closed the diary, holding it tightly shut with her hands. He seemed so *nice*. He had spiky thick hair and he'd talked about her mum in a real way. Laughing at her silly habits; her text messages, her leather jacket, her lack of punctuality. When he spoke about her there was affection in his voice.

She tossed the diary on to the bed. Amid her annoyance there was a creeping feeling of shame. Had that been it? His reason for coming to see her? What had she thought? That he *fancied* her? Desired her? When all the time he had come to nose around in her mum's things.

The derelict house in Warwick Lane was the eighth home Nicky had lived in. He took his cross and chain out of its box and held it for a few moments, letting the chain slide between his fingers. It was precious to him and yet he had never worn it. He doubted he ever would.

He looked round the room. It was lighter now than when he had first found it. Over the weeks of watching he'd used his Swiss Army knife to gouge small chunks of wood out of the boards that covered the windows. There were about eight eyelet holes spaced out, where the sun speared through. It gave the room a kind of dappled light and Nicky felt comfortable sitting there. If he needed to read he could either pull back the loose board on the window or, if it was overcast, he could use his torch. The previous couple of nights he had lit three or four candles and placed them on saucers on the floor. Enough light for him to see the four corners of the room. He had to be careful though; he couldn't afford to use too many candles in case someone noticed.

He didn't think any of the neighbours would. It was the kind of street where people went about their business and hardly seemed to notice what was going on a few feet away under their noses.

How different it was to the first house he remembered living in with Lindy and Terry Shields. After a first attempt at adoption had broken down he was placed in foster care with the Shields. Their house had been tiny, one of a terrace in the outskirts of Norwich. Looking out of his bedroom window on to the tiny back yard he could have rubbed elbows with the kids next door when they were doing the same thing. The living room and kitchen were all in one, with a long sofa that took up a whole chunk of the wall. The middle of it sagged but the arms still sat up rigidly. Nicky used to stand on one end and pretend he was on the bow of a ship. He had a toy telescope and he looked through it as though he was searching for sharks.

Terry Shields had a pirate hat which he wore to join in with the game and he would creep along the floor and pretend to climb up on to the deck and have sword fights with Nicky.

Terry was a giant, Nicky knew that because he had to duck going through doorways in case he bumped his head. His stomach was big and when he laughed it wobbled like a huge jelly. When he sat on one end of the sofa the other end lifted off the floor a couple of centimetres. Nicky and Lindy always sat heavily on it to try and balance him. He drove a 92 single-decker bus and sometimes Lindy would take Nicky for a ride on it and they'd sit in the nearest seat to the driver. They wouldn't have to pay because Terry would just wink at them and wave them by his cubicle while he stamped out tickets for the real passengers. Sometimes Nicky imagined that the bus was a proud sailing ship and Terry was the captain. As it splashed through the streets Nicky saw himself as an explorer looking for new lands.

Lindy was quite plump as well.

'I'm a size sixteen, darling, but I'm looking good.'

And Nicky thought she was. She had red hair that was stiff with lacquer and she wore orange lipstick and false eyelashes. They lay in a plastic box like two spiders and every time she and Terry went out to the pub she sat in front of a mirror and let Nicky watch as she stuck them on. Before she left she always gave Nicky a giant hug and he seemed to disappear between her huge soft breasts.

He called them Mum and Dad even though they explained to him that they weren't really his parents. He was content in that tiny house where the next-door neighbours were in and out and where people borrowed each other's tools and baking trays. He was happiest lying on the ship-sofa waiting for Terry or Lindy to read him a bedtime story.

'Let's get this cabin boy up to bed!' Terry would say and hoist Nicky up on to his shoulders to climb the stairs, stooping all the time in case Nicky hit his head on the ceiling.

Then one day Terry Shields had a heart attack and died. Everyone in the street cried and Lindy stopped wearing the lipstick and the false eyelashes.

He'd been at the wheel of his bus when it happened. It was just after the shopping centre stop and all the passengers had paid and were sitting down waiting for the bus to move off up the road. It just sat there, though, and the traffic sailed round it. People started to mumble and complain after a few minutes but nobody went up to see what was wrong.

Nicky had never understood how that could be. One minute Terry was warm and pink, his eyes creasing up with laughter, his fingers running through his hair. Then there was nothing. An empty seat at the front of a 92 bus that had been washed up at the side of a one-way road.

For some reason Lindy hadn't been able to look after Nicky any longer after that, and he'd been placed in the local authority home where he'd lived for a while *waiting for the right parents to come along.*

Nicky put the cross and chain back in its box. He remembered the social worker ('*call me Barbara*') who had given it to him.

'You might want to keep this, Nicky,' she'd said, after a long and stuttering explanation.

He was only seven but he understood everything she had said. It explained why he had no parents of his own and had to live with people he had no connection with. It also explained why he was called *Nicholas Nelson.*

Nicky pushed the board aside and looked out of the window at Chloe's house. There was no sign of her or her dad. Part of him wanted to get up and walk across the street and knock on her door. *Hi*, he might say, *I was just passing.* They could chat like they had before, and maybe he would reach out and run his finger down her arm, or use his hand to stop her hair flying away in wisps.

He slumped back against the wall. He knew he wouldn't do it, *couldn't* do it. It gave him a melancholy feeling and he began to feel sleepy. In front of him were hazy strips of sunlight like silk ribbons pinned from one corner of the room to the other. He closed his eyes for a moment. How peaceful it was there. How right he had been to move to somewhere of his own.

The next foster-parents he had were the Talbots. Anne

and Tony who lived outside Lowestoft with their twin girls. He'd been nine when they'd taken him on. He'd had problems in school and wet the bed from time to time but they'd been kind and sweet, especially Anne, who read with him and helped him with his maths. The twins were in their teens and liked having a younger brother around to look after and boss around and he hadn't minded. After some months the bed-wetting stopped and he was settled. They called him *Nicholas*, making his name sound posh. He'd been happy there.

Then Tony got a job in Germany. It was unexpected, out of the blue. The money and prospects were good and he couldn't turn it down. It was only for two years. Nicholas could go with them. Why not?

It didn't happen, though, and Nicky never really understood why. On the day that his social worker came to take him away he got ready early and sat on the bottom stair with his coat on and his bags packed beside him. Anne and Tony and the twins assured him that when they came back he could come and live with them again *Although*, Tony said, *they'll probably have found you a really nice mum and dad by then*. As though it was just a case of looking round the next corner.

Then it was back to another council home and then another. Nicky dismissed them from his thoughts; they were forgettable. Unlike the Marshall family. He would never forget his time there.

He stood up, shaking the thoughts away. It was better

to keep his mind off the past. He squatted down at his rucksack and pulled out a magazine. Then he settled down to read.

Chloe picked up the handset and dialled the number for Crystal House.

'Can I speak to Nicky Nelson?' she said politely, her fingers tapping lightly on the hall table.

'Who wants him?' a young male voice said.

'Is he there?' she said. 'It's a friend.'

'Hang on.'

There were some loud voices in the background. Eventually the voice at the other end came back and said, 'Nicky's gone.'

'Gone out?' Chloe said. 'Any idea when he'll be back?'

It was a silly question. As though the kids in Crystal House kept tabs on each other.

'No, he's gone. Done a bunk. Left.'

'Oh!'

'Don't s'pose he'll come back. Sorry.'

The line went dead and Chloe was left holding the handset at her ear. She was too late. Nicky had gone.

14

Chloe could hear her dad moving around upstairs. He was getting ready to go out. He'd decided to go to football training, something he did every year at this time; getting ready for the football season. She'd been surprised when he told her. She'd known he was getting better. He was looking so crisp and organized. It gave her a strange feeling. She should have been pleased but instead she felt a sort of panic. It was as if he was moving away from her; as if he was in a car that was disappearing in the distance and she was left standing by the road.

She got up off the futon and stood at the French doors. Even though it was almost seven it was still hot. She pushed them open as far as they would go. There were blocks of shadow in the back garden, the sun sinking low for the evening. Over by the gate there was an old bike that her dad had picked up at a house he was working on. One of its tyres was completely flat and it looked rusted in places.

The phone call to Crystal House had left her deflated. It had taken her a while to build up the courage. The fact that Nicky wasn't there, that he was no longer at the home, had thrown her into confusion.

The day before he had he left abruptly, rudely. Then there were the missing diary pages. Heavy in her mind was the letter and the photograph. Among all these things she had suddenly thought of the broken window, weeks before, on the day of her mum's funeral.

She'd wanted to talk to him, to hear his voice. But in his absence it was beginning to seem likely that he had done all these things. Yet his face, his attitude, his friendliness, his touch; these things contradicted this. How could this person be capable of such nastiness?

Her mum would have been able to explain. *Many of these kids are damaged. They're hard work, they're unpleasant, rude, sometimes they're downright scary.* She'd heard her mum talk like this a lot. The children she looked after were difficult, damaged. *A lot of their behaviour is attention seeking. They've not had a lot of that in their lives so they do things which demand that people notice them, giving them the attention they want.*

Was Nicky Nelson seeking attention? What if Chloe gave him that attention? Might he not open up to her? Tell her if and why he was angry with her mum?

She was making it sound like a completely selfless act; as though she was the *social worker* and he was her client. As though she had no further interest in him than that. But the truth was she was attracted to him and it made her feel bad. How could she have feelings for *anyone* when she was still saying goodbye to her mum? It felt like a betrayal. Was there an amount of time, she wondered, after which it was all right to go back to living a normal life?

Anyway, she had always been hopeless when it came to boys. She had no brothers. Her mum and dad had no siblings either so she had no cousins. At school she'd buried her head in her books and hung round with girls who showed no interest. How was she to know if Nicky was really attracted to her? Or if he had other motives.

Hearing her dad's footsteps coming down the stairs, she stood up and stretched her arms up to the ceiling. She should pull herself together. She picked up a prospectus and was holding it in her hand when her dad came in, looking relaxed, carrying a hold-all. He frowned momentarily at the disarray in the room.

'I think I'll move back to my bedroom tomorrow,' she said.

'Good. We need to get back to normal.'

Normal. The word hung uncomfortably between them. Her dad cleared his throat.

'I shouldn't be too late. In this heat we won't be playing for too long. I did say I might go to the pub afterwards. Will you be all right?'

'Course,' she said. 'I'll just watch telly. I might have an early night.'

She heard the front door close and sat looking around the room. The night stretched ahead of her. The bootlace cat had appeared as if from nowhere. It leapt gracefully on to her bed and lay down. The cat who was hated once was now a comfort.

Her mum would have seen the funny side of that.

Nicky was too tense by far. He'd watched Chloe's father leave the house carrying a hold-all. The man appeared quite jaunty. He'd tossed his car keys into the air and caught them again.

It meant that Chloe was on her own. As soon as he realized this he became agitated. He wanted to go and see her. It made him walk up and down the room, his mobile in his hand. He had Lesley's home phone number, had found it weeks ago. He could ring her. Ask if he could go over. Why not?

The very thought unsettled him. He sat down on the floor, his back against the wall. Why? Did he want to see her to hurt her in some way? Or to just *be* with her again? That was the problem. He didn't know. He found that he'd put his mobile up to his mouth and he was banging it lightly against his lips. If only he could calm down, relax, take a composed look at the situation.

Relax, why don't you just relax!

The face of Ben Marshall materialized in his head. The wonderful Ben, seventeen-year-old son of the Marshalls. Nicky pushed the back of his head against the wall. The Marshalls. The last family he had lived with. It wasn't something he liked to remember but sometimes it wasn't possible to blank out the pictures.

He was almost sixteen when he landed at the Marshalls' front door. Lesley had driven him there in her car and told him all about them.

'Helen and Patrick are both teachers. He's a senior teacher and she works part time. They're really nice people. They've fostered a few children over the years for us and virtually all the placements worked out well. They've got a son of their own, Ben. He's just a bit older than you. A bit of a computer nerd but a nice enough lad. You play your cards right, Nicky, and you could make a home for yourself here.'

After Lesley had gone, Helen showed Nicky to his room.

'The room next door is Ben's. You'll get on well with him. And don't be worried about the fact that Patrick is a senior teacher. He's a pussy-cat at home. You ask any of the kids who have stayed with us. They'll tell you.'

Helen was always saying that: *You ask anyone and they'll tell you.* Whether it was about the price of bread or the low pay of teachers. She was a smiley sort of woman who liked to fill all silences with a lot of talk. Nicky supposed it was because she lived in a house with two males, neither of whom said a lot.

Patrick, it turned out, had left all his authority at school and at home was a softie. A big man, with a red face and a round stomach; he reminded Nicky of Father Christmas off season. He was always behind a large newspaper and whenever Nicky was around gave him a wink and said, *All right, lad? Ask me if there's anything you want.* Nicky couldn't help but like the man who often rolled his eyes in his direction when Helen was grumbling about something.

Ben was something else. He was a temperamental lad with longish hair and big sad eyes. One minute he was jokey and nice and the next he sank into a black mood which seemed to take hours to dissolve. At first that was all that worried Nicky: how to tell what sort of form Ben was in; how to avoid getting his head bitten off if Ben was gloomy.

It's his hormones, Helen said over and over. *You ask anyone and they'll tell you.*

In the first weeks living there he'd spent a fair bit of time working with Patrick in the garage. The big man had set up a workshop in there with a bench and racks of tools hanging along the wall. He showed Nicky how to make stuff; shelves for his room, a bedside table. *Ben tried to do this but he's all fingers and thumbs! He's much more at home in front of a keyboard.* Patrick had said.

The fact that Nicky was spending a lot of time with Patrick didn't seem to bother Ben at all. Leaning into Nicky's room, he eyed the shelves and the table and drew a long sigh.

'The old man got you making stuff, then?' he said, and walked away without further comment.

When he was in a good mood he was like a different person. He insisted that Nicky come in and work on the computer. Nicky was impressed. It was a powerful machine and had all the latest attachments and gadgets. It was linked up to the internet and Ben showed him how to log on and search for music websites. He organized a personal email address for Nicky and showed him how to master the graphics so that he could use it for his homework.

Sitting directly behind Nicky on a second chair, Ben often let his hand or arm rest on Nicky's shoulder while he was pointing to the screen or showing him what to do. The whole thing was complicated and Ben reached across to help out, his arm brushing by Nicky's, his breath hot on Nicky's neck or cheek.

That was how it started.

Nicky stood up, brushing the dust off his jeans. He walked across to the window. He wanted to make sure that Chloe didn't go out. He liked the fact that she was there, across the road, just moments away from him. If he wanted he could go there. If he didn't he could leave her alone. The choice was his. He was in charge.

At the Marshalls he had never been in control.

One day Ben was there at his shoulder and Nicky felt comfortable. *Wanted*. The next day the older boy's hand was rubbing up and down Nicky's thigh, his breaths quickening, his eyes shutting out Nicky's panic and distaste. *Relax!* he'd whispered. *Why don't you just relax!*

Nicky swallowed the dryness out of his throat and tried to loosen the muscles at the back of his neck. He moved his head from side to side and lifted the wood from the window to let the air trickle in. He heard a faint cheer in the distance. The sound shook him from his thoughts. He concentrated and listened hard. He pictured a group of boys playing with a ball under the streetlights; passing it to each other, calling out names, making jokes, a surge of delight as one of them scored a goal. He felt a stab of envy that seemed to turn in his ribs. He had never been like that: one of lads, out in the street hanging around, with nothing more to worry about than where the next can of Coke was coming from or who was going to get hold of the next packet of fags. He had always been an outsider: last in class, new kid in a family, recent arrival in a council home. He'd gravitated towards the other loners: odd kids who couldn't get on with anybody, the fat, the thin, the boffins, the dimwits, the villains; he'd hung around with all of them. No easy-going football games for them, just little knots of tension huddling in the corner of a playground.

That was why Ben's friendship had been important. Ben's dark moods made his good humour, his warmth, all the more special when it happened. That's why he didn't move away when Ben gave him a playful hug; that's why he didn't refuse to sit on the bed beside the older boy when he had a new computer magazine that they both could look at. And when Ben's hand rested on his leg or played with his hair he just sort of ignored it.

The rest, the holding, the touching; those things happened over time.

Nicky felt his jaw begin to tremble. He had to stop thinking like this. He glanced down and saw his mobile in his hand, Lesley's telephone number across the screen. Not Lesley's any more. Chloe's number. He wanted to ring it; he was ready to ring it.

Lesley had known something was wrong at the Marshalls'. She had asked him several times, *You're not yourself, Nicky. What's up?* In the end he'd given her stories about not fitting into school or worrying about his exams. He'd also hinted that Ben's moods came from a mild jealousy and he was dealing with it himself. *Don't say anything to Patrick or Helen*, he'd said and she had assured him that she wouldn't. He'd given her a fiction and she'd accepted it.

So what if Ben was a bit too friendly? It was probably an adolescent thing and he would grow out of it. It was the price he had to pay for having his own room in a nice house with Patrick and Helen.

Patrick and Helen; he was big and round, the belt of his trousers curving underneath his stomach, the buttons on his shirt straining to stay put. When he was in the garage doing woodwork he slid his pencil behind his ear and put his tape measure in his shirt pocket. Helen was tall and stringy, her clothes always looking as though they were one size too big; the neck gaping, the sleeves covering half her hand, the trousers loose and baggy. They were a seaside postcard couple but that didn't matter. They liked Nicky and he felt comfortable with them.

If things had stayed the same he could have coped. But they didn't. Remembering it made Nicky feel light-headed. His eyes felt like tiny sharp pebbles and he closed his lids and let them bathe in the darkness.

That day, in Ben's bedroom, it was to be the last time but Nicky hadn't known that then. He'd sat on the bed next to Ben. He'd even undone his own clothes and rested his head back against the pillow. He watched as if from a distance as the older boy's face took on a look of intensity, then his expression changed and he looked as though he was in a trance.

Nicky was disgusted. In his throat there was bile and he swallowed it back and steeled himself for the moment when it was over, when he could get up and go back to his room, leaving Ben lying weak and exhausted across his duvet.

But the door opened. Patrick stood there looking at the two of them. It was a shock to see the big man, his head bent slightly, his hand leaning on the door frame. Nicky could feel the panic in his own face as his jaw began to twitch. He wanted to say, *This is nothing to do with me! This is not my fault! I didn't start this!* But his tongue just fluttered in his mouth like a lost bird. Patrick stood in the doorway, his face solemn; whether it was anger or sadness he hadn't been able to tell. Nicky put his hand on Ben's shoulder and shook it roughly. Ben looked up and saw his father. Then he sat up stiffly and moved away and Nicky pulled at the waistband of his jeans.

Nicky would never forget Patrick's face, his expression unreadable, his eyes like slits, looking at him. Accusing *him*.

He stood up and walked to the far end of the empty room, his feet sounding on the floorboards. He would stop thinking about it. When he could walk no further he pushed his face into the wall, smelling the dampness of the paper. He found himself choking back a sob, gasping for breath. It hadn't been his fault, any of it.

After a moment he turned round and walked back towards the window. All the time he felt his thumb jerking across the keys of his mobile. He'd ring Chloe. Go over there. Why not? The screen lit up. He put his mobile to his ear and suddenly her voice was there. He coughed.

'Chloe, it's Nicky. I was going to come round.'

She told him her dad had gone out; she said she was clearing her room; she talked on, her words a light bubbly stream. When she paused he spoke.

'In about ten, fifteen minutes?'

He cut the call. He'd done it now. It had pushed all that other stuff – the Marshalls – from his mind. A calm feeling came over him like a cool breeze. He sat down again, feeling better. The memories had been shut away again. That was where they belonged.

15

He didn't come. An hour after his call she finally gave up.

Why had he bothered to phone? To make the arrangement?

Something made her open the front door and go out into the street. She looked up and down. He wasn't coming. He was just playing with her. It made her feel stupid, especially as she'd changed her clothes. Instead of her usual jeans she'd put a skirt and a T-shirt on. It had made her feel good, the fabric touching her skin, her legs bare beneath. She'd come downstairs after changing and felt like someone on her way out to a party.

Stupid. She was just no good with boys.

The sound of the telephone ringing made her run back inside the house. If it was him she was going to tell him to get lost.

'Hello?' she said, breathlessly.

It was her gran.

'Oh hi!' she said, masking the disappointment in her voice.

Her gran started talking about the heat. The beach was as hot as a frying pan and people were going to casualty with sunburn.

'It's hot here . . .' Chloe started but her gran continued talking. Prince and Queenie were out of sorts and every time Sonia came in from a shopping trip she looked like she'd been in a sauna. By the way, Sonia's mother, Vera, had passed away. Bless her. It was a relief because the old lady had been ill for years.

'I'm sorry,' Chloe said.

But Gran carried on. Lowestoft was in the record books for having the driest August for fifty years and no one was allowed to use a hosepipe. Her gran did, though, every night at eleven o'clock. Everyone else did so why shouldn't she?

While her gran was talking, something clicked in Chloe's thoughts. *Lowestoft.* That's where her mum went to meet with a social worker about Nicky Nelson. Those were the pages that had been torn out of the diary. When her gran finally paused to take a breath she suddenly said, 'Gran, did Mum ever talk to you about one of her cases. A boy called Nicky Nelson?'

There was a small silence.

'Nicky Nelson?' Her gran finally repeated the name.

'Yes, a lad she was looking after. She had a meeting in Lowestoft in April and I wondered if she'd come round to see you.'

'Why'd you ask?'

'I just wondered. Only I was picking Mum's stuff up and I met him . . .'

But her gran's dogs had started barking and there was a commotion.

'I've got someone at the door, petal. I'll call you back in the next couple of days.'

Chloe replaced the handset. The house was quiet as a church. In the distance she could hear a cheer, as if a game was going on and someone had scored a goal. She walked into the back dining room and felt the heat. Standing at the French doors, she looked out into the garden. She could smell a barbecue from somewhere nearby and hear the distant tinkle of music.

It was only nine-thirty but she felt sleepy. Long hot days of doing almost nothing were making her feel tired all the time. It would have to stop. Tomorrow she would move her stuff back upstairs into her own bedroom and later on in the day she would go out; shopping or to the library or maybe she would call on one of her friends.

She lay down on the bed. She reached across and clicked on the fan. It came on immediately and wafted a light breeze across her, turning its face from side to side in a slow rhythmic movement. Her skirt rippled and she felt the cool air on her toes.

She felt better. Her plans gave her a sudden feeling of calm. The business with Nicky was beyond her. How could it be any other way? A sudden movement made her rise up, startled. It was the bootlace cat again, landing gracefully on the duvet. It sat beside her, stretching out, arching its back in her direction. Using her thumb she caressed the back of the cat's ears. She had a vague notion that she might read but actually she just lay, stroking the animal, her mind blank. She knew she was falling asleep but she didn't stop herself. After a few minutes her eyelids closed.

Nicky stood in the corner of Chloe's garden next to an old rusted bike. It was dark except for the light spilling out from the French doors. He wondered what he was doing there. A cat sprang out of the room and walked delicately across the lawn and disappeared into the bushes. Taking care not to make a noise Nicky moved towards the house. The French doors were open. He could see her lying on the bed. She was asleep. A lamp by the bed threw a dull light across her. A fan was blowing, causing a ripple on the fabric of her skirt. The sight of her touched him. He only hesitated for a moment then he stepped inside.

16

Lesley Cozens's dining room was about the same size as his room in the derelict house but it looked smaller. Nicky had been in it before but this time he noticed how full up it was. A big old cupboard at the far end was packed full of cups and saucers. There were a couple of armchairs that didn't match and the bed was low and modern. It seemed as though there was hardly enough space for him to stand up. By his side was an old dining table.

He watched Chloe for a few moments and wondered what he was supposed to be doing. Why hadn't he just knocked on the front door, why had he crept in like a thief? He breathed slowly. Glancing down to the table he saw a pile of what looked like university prospectuses. His shoulders slumped. Everywhere he looked there seemed to be some reminder.

Patrick Marshall had been in charge of the careers department at his school and their house had always been awash with college and university materials. That very year Ben had been looking for the right college to go to. Oxford or Cambridge; maybe Sussex or Durham. He had the grades. He was a bright boy. He would get on.

Nicky looked away, his eyes closing for a second. Blanking the prospectuses from his thoughts he turned his head and concentrated on Chloe. She looked peaceful, her body still, her chest rising and falling. It made him feel tired to look at her. His face felt heavy, his arms and hands like dead weights. He took a step across to the bed and lowered himself down until he was sitting on it. He leant forward, his elbows on his knees, his head in his hands.

Behind him Chloe continued to sleep.

What was he doing there?

He rubbed his eyes. He wasn't there at all, not really. In his head he was back in Ben's room on that last day when Patrick had found them together. Nicky in a state of undress; Ben sitting up suddenly, a startled expression on his face. Patrick standing there, filling the doorway, as if he was about to preach a sermon.

He didn't do that though. He pointed at his own son and then made a thumbing gesture to tell him to get out of the room. Ben was gone before Nicky could open his mouth.

'What the hell is going on?' Patrick said.

It's not my fault, Nicky wanted to say. Instead he moved along Ben's bed, up to the corner, and dragged the duvet towards himself. Patrick walked across and pulled out the chair to Ben's desk and sat on it, a great sigh coming from him.

How could Nicky explain? He would have to blame

Ben, he would have to say that it had been going on for weeks, that Ben had started it, that Ben was the one who initiated it every time, that he hated it and wished it had never happened.

'What have you got to say for yourself?' Patrick said, looking tired.

Nicky noticed a small stubby pencil behind Patrick's ear. Then he saw a slither of wood stuck under Patrick's belt, the type that came from planing a surface. Patrick was making something. The floor in the garage was probably covered in curls of wood. Misery settled on him. He could have been down there, in the workshop helping him; instead he had been lying on Ben's wrinkled duvet, his body like jelly, weak and malleable, allowing himself to be used. What sort of person was he?

'Have you got nothing to say for yourself?' Patrick said, his big girth slumping in the swivel chair.

Nicky shook his head and Patrick looked away from him, his eyes moving around the room. In a low voice Patrick started to talk about what had happened. Nicky closed his eyes with shame. He couldn't answer any questions, he couldn't say a word. He knew what would happen. Patrick would talk to his son and Ben would blame it on him and he would be told to leave. What could Nicky say that would be believed? He was a boy who had been in and out of different homes all his life. What was his word worth up against Patrick's own son? The big friendly man would order him to pack his bag and then Lesley would arrive. Patrick would tell her everything and she would know what he had been doing. He would tell her how he found Nicky on Ben's bed abusing the trust that he'd been given, taking advantage of the son of the family. How would it look? He'd make excuses, of course he would. He had simply gone along with it so that he could stay with the family. But Patrick was Ben's real father. He wouldn't want to see that. Blood was thicker, Nicky knew that. Blood was like a sticky glue that held people together. This thought filled him with sadness and he started to cry, tiny sobs that squeezed out of his mouth and made his chin tremble.

'Look, lad,' Patrick said, 'I've said my piece and I don't want to hear another word about this. I want you to stay away from Ben. Most of all I don't want Helen to know about this, do you understand?'

Nicky stopped crying. He frowned. What was he hearing? That it was all right? That he wasn't going to be sent away? He didn't understand.

'Just stay away from Ben,' Patrick said, standing up, the chair creaking under him.

Then he left.

Chloe was snoring softly. Nicky looked round at her. How simple it would be to lie down, to fall into a deep sleep. He lay back on the bed, his head on her pillow. He felt stiff and awkward but he turned towards her so that they were lying in spoons. He felt like a block of wood though, his shoulders like right angles, his spine in a straight line. Chloe was the opposite. He put his arm around her waist. She was still asleep, her body warm and limp. It was as if he could do anything with her.

Just like Ben had done with him.

Nicky buried his face in Chloe's hair. He could smell the shampoo and sleep from her. Then he pulled her as close as he could.

Chloe's eyes opened and blinked into the light. Instantly she felt an arm around her, clamping her to the spot. The fan was still whirring and she realized with a sudden feeling of panic that she was being held down, pinned to one place; that someone was there in the room, behind her on the bed.

'What? What?'

Her voice was high-pitched and her breaths were shallow and quick. She should call out, scream out, but the grip around her waist was tight.

'Let go, let go . . .' she half shouted, moving her legs around, trying to kick behind her.

'Chloe . . . It's all right.'

The words were muffled. He was talking into the back of her neck, his hot breath on her skin. She knew the voice. Nicky Nelson, lying behind her, holding her. No, *restraining* her.

'Let me go . . .'

'Relax,' he said hoarsely, one of his legs moving across her, pinning her down to the bed.

'What do you want?' she said, her voice cracking.

She tried to turn, to face him, and just ended up on her back with his leg and arm across her. She was breathing heavily, her hands in fists, lifting her trunk and lowering it again. He raised himself up from her neck and looked at her, his face glazed, his eyes like dark beads. He didn't look like himself.

'Let me go,' she said, weakly.

'Ssh,' he said and then brought his face down.

He was going to kiss her. She shook her head vehemently.

'No!' she shouted, her voice gaining strength.

'Ssh,' he said, moving across so that he was half on top of her, his weight flattening her. 'I'm not going to hurt you. I just want to hold you. I just want . . .'

His knee was between her legs and he was pressing himself on to her. She could feel him hard and determined.

'Don't do this,' she said as he pushed his hand inside her T-shirt and pulled himself up so that he was lying directly on top of her.

'Just relax!' he said, his words hard, his knees between her legs.

He kissed her hard, his body pressing down on her, his hand pushing her skirt up, his breathing fast. He was *excited*. It made her feel sick. She pulled her mouth away from him.

'Nicky, Nicky, don't do this, don't do it. NICKY!' she screamed.

He stopped abruptly and pulled back. He was startled, as if he'd been in some sort of trance. Then his features changed, softened, as if he'd only just recognized her.

'You're hurting me. Get off. Please let me go!'

He looked down and seemed surprised at where he was, what he was doing. He took his hand from under her skirt and rolled back so that she was free to move. She scrambled off the bed and stood by the window, her arms across her chest. By the side of her the French doors were open. She could go out if she wanted to but something stopped her.

'What's going on?' she said, angrily.

He backed away from her. He looked as if he was lost.

Nicky stepped away from the bed and stood in front of the big cupboard. It was packed to the edges with cups and saucers. There were other things as well; jugs and bowls and vases, not a spare inch of space. The sight of it overwhelmed him and his breaths were shallow. As if he were in there, wedged in without any room to move.

'What's the matter, Nicky?'

Chloe's voice came from behind him. She used his name softly. *Nicky. Nicky.* Not a name someone had ever given him. Just a convenience; just a way of identifying him.

Then she was beside him, her hand on his arm.

'Nicky, what's wrong? Is it to do with my mum?' she said, her hand rubbing up and down his arm.

He began to bang his knuckles together. Why couldn't he be like her? *Kind? Forgiving?*

'Relax, Nicky,' she whispered. 'Relax.'

Relax, why don't you just relax! It was Ben again. Always there. Always in his head.

'Get off. GET OFF!' he burst out, pushing Chloe away, and then, using his hands like battering rams, he punched at the glass in the cupboard. Sudden pains shot up through his wrists and he stood back and pulled open the doors and swept the shelves of the cups and the saucers, each of them tumbling and crashing out. Chloe retreated, an expression of astonishment on her face, looking at the glass and china cascading on to the floor.

Then he stopped and turned to her, his hands held out in front of him. He could see her expression. Fear, pity, disgust. She was looking at his hands, the blood welling out of his torn skin.

'Leave me alone!' he said, kicking out at the debris on the floor.

Cradling his hands, he sidestepped Chloe and he walked out of the room.

* * *

Chloe moved towards the cupboard, her shoulders and arms shaking, her head nodding frantically with suppressed sobs. She looked down at the wreckage on the floor. Her mother's cups and saucers; smashed into pieces.

17

Her dad started to clear up the glass and crockery while waiting for the police to arrive. He was on his knees with the hand brush and dustpan. Chloe could hear the broken bits grating along the floor as he swept them up and the rattle as they dropped into an old plastic box. He was grumbling quietly under his breath, *I shouldn't have gone out. I should have stayed at home.*

She was sitting on the corner of the bed, her back to the place where she'd been lying twenty minutes earlier. She was still shaken, her fingers playing with the fabric of her top; her mouth was dry, her eyes were sore at the corners from where she'd rubbed them.

She hadn't told her dad the truth. She'd said that she'd been upstairs in the bathroom when she'd heard the sound of glass smashing. By the time she'd got downstairs the room was empty.

'Were the French doors open?'

She nodded.

'I told you not to leave the doors open!'

'It was so hot . . .' she started, but felt the tears coming back.

Her dad put the dustpan down and came across to the bed and gave her a hug.

'Whoever it was just hit out at this,' her dad said, pointing to the shattered cupboard. 'They didn't take anything?'

She shook her head.

'I don't understand.'

She wouldn't tell him about Nicky. She couldn't explain what had happened without it sounding as if Nicky were completely out of control, and she didn't want to do that. *Many of these kids are damaged . . . sometimes they're downright scary*, her mum had said. She remembered the phrase *attention seeking*. Why was Nicky trying to get her attention? What did he want? This was something she couldn't tell her dad. He simply wouldn't understand.

There was no police siren, just the ring of the door bell and then the sound of heavy footsteps coming down the hall to the back dining room where Chloe was still sitting on the bed. The older policeman, whose hair was thin and combed across his scalp, took one look at the French doors and tutted as if they were to blame. Then he leant wearily against the wall and left the interview to the other policeman.

He was younger, his hair closely cut into his scalp looking prickly, like the bristles of a brush. He sat down close to her with his notepad. She noticed that one of his fingernails had gone black as though he'd closed it in a door. He looked earnestly at her and told her to take her time and tell him what had happened. He only wrote on his pad when she'd finished a sentence and he didn't look irritated when she kept going back and starting again.

'And you didn't see anybody?' he said, looking up at her dad.

She shook her head.

The policeman nodded in a satisfied manner. He seemed to make a couple of ticks in his book and a lot of notes. Every now and again he threw a sad look over at the broken bits on the floor. When he got up to leave, the other policeman walked across to the French doors and rattled them as though to test the lock.

'Well, we'll be in touch,' the younger man said, giving her a friendly nod.

They left leaflets about Victim Support and Chloe held on to them, her eyes blurring when she tried to focus on the words. Her dad sat beside her. He was in his track suit bottoms and T-shirt and smelled of deodorant and soap. He'd arrived home only minutes after Nicky left. They could have passed each other in the street.

'Chloe, love. I feel sick to my stomach about this. When I think of what might have—'

'Nothing happened to me,' Chloe interrupted, gesturing towards the cupboard, the broken glass and empty shelves, 'just Mum's things.'

She pictured Nicky standing in front of the cupboard looking down at his hands. The blood, she remembered, oozed out, looking thick and dark.

'I'm going to ring Gran,' her dad said, in a determined tone. 'I don't want you round here while I'm out at work. I want you out of the way.'

Chloe heard him out in the hallway. He was punching numbers on to the receiver and then there was a mumble as he spoke to her gran. The noise became more distant as he walked further up the hallway out of earshot. Chloe looked at the glass in the plastic box glinting under the electric light. All her mum's china. Her mum. Lesley Cozens. *After you and Dad my job is the most important thing in my life. It needs to be for these kids. They have no one to look out for them. They have parents who abuse them, discard them. When they come to us they're broken apart. We try to put them back together.*

Something had gone wrong in Nicky Nelson's case. He was still in pieces and he blamed her mum for it.

'Your gran's fine with that,' her dad said, coming back into the room.

He stood looking directly at the cupboard, avoiding catching her eye. He was at a loss. He didn't know what to do. Then he seemed to pull himself together and squatted down to look more closely at the damage. The glass doors were ruined but the rest of it was untouched. He walked out to the kitchen and then came back in with his tape measure. Grabbing a piece of paper from the table and a pen from his pocket he began to take measurements. He looked as though he was in charge again. Chloe had an image of him the next day; he would have his toolbox and some new panes of glass and he would set about mending the cupboard. He would restore it the way that her mum would have done. Except for the china. Some things just couldn't be mended.

'In the morning I'll drive you to Lowestoft. Then at least I'll know that you're safe. You can come back when school starts.'

She opened her mouth to speak but her dad's face had closed over. He had made his plans. He had decided. She would go to Lowestoft and stay with her gran.

18

Nicky looked out through the loose board and saw the policemen returning to their car. One of them got into the driver's seat and the other was about to follow when he looked directly up towards Nicky, towards the derelict house.

He ducked back, letting the wooden board fall across the window. He sat absolutely still, hardly breathing, wondering if the policeman was going to walk across the road and come into the old house. He didn't dare look out of the window again so he listened hard.

There were sounds from the front garden: the old gate opening, footsteps along the path, then a loud noise as the front door was pushed. It didn't open; of course it wouldn't, there was a padlock on the inside. A couple more rattles and the policeman seemed to give up and Nicky heard his footsteps receding. The slam of a car door and the sound of the engine starting gave Nicky the courage to look out once more. The police car disappeared up the street. He slumped back against the wall, his heart hardly beating at all, the back of his neck aching with tension.

After a few minutes he went back to the far corner of the room where, with some difficulty, he lit half a dozen candles. His sleeping bag was unzipped and he sat down on it and pulled it around his legs. Even though it was a sultry evening he felt cold. He held his hands up in the light. There was just one cut on the right hand, near the knuckle. It was painful but it had stopped bleeding. His left hand was another matter; there were at least four cuts that he could see and a couple of them seemed quite deep. He'd tried winding a pale cotton T-shirt around it but the blood was still soaking through.

He really needed to go to hospital but he knew that there would be questions asked. Most likely some pleasant nurse would slip out and telephone the police or social services while he was having his stitches done and he would be picked up and taken back to Crystal House. Then there would be the third degree from Trevor. The thought of it made him feel weak. Trevor would want to know why he did it; why he tried to force himself on Lesley's daughter. Then the police would be called.

How could he explain any of it?

Like when he first left the Marshalls' and everyone was asking him why he had hurt Ben. An unprovoked attack, they had called it. He had never told anyone though. He'd just shrugged his shoulders as if he couldn't explain.

When Patrick left him that day and the door of Ben's bedroom had shut he lay with his face buried in Ben's duvet. He had no tears, just shame. He seemed to shrink into the bedding, to become smaller, thinner, less substantial. In the middle of it all was a troubled feeling of gratitude. Patrick wasn't going to send him back. He just wanted it to stop, for him to stay away from Ben.

The sound of the bedroom door opening startled him. He looked up and saw Ben.

'The old man give you a bad time?' he said, coming towards him, looking as though he was going to sit on the bed.

Nicky clambered up, stepping backwards to the door, putting as much distance between them as he could.

'Don't come near me,' he said, his voice so low it sounded like a growl.

Ben made a *huh!* sound. It made Nicky angry.

'You hear what I said. You come near me and I'll hurt you.'

Ben made no move in Nicky's direction. He looked him up and down. Nicky felt the boy's eyes travelling across his body.

'What's the old man said, Nicky? You don't want to take any notice of him! It's not like you're the *first* person he's had a little talk with.'

Ben's words threw him off track.

'I don't understand,' he said, pushing his anger down, trying to work out what was being said.

'Don't be jealous, mate . . .' Ben said dismissively, turning towards the computer. 'Why don't we go on line . . .'

But Nicky felt a sudden rage inside him. It gusted through him, cold and raw, and his arms and legs tensed up and his fists formed.

'Play a game?' Ben said, giving him a throwaway smile as if nothing had happened.

Nicky squared up. He felt bigger, taller, stronger than the older boy. No longer the crumpled mess that had hidden in the duvet but someone who shouldn't be pushed around.

'All right?' Ben said tentatively, his hand reaching out to touch Nicky's shoulder.

That was it. The touch that did it. Like pulling a trigger it set off something in Nicky that couldn't be stopped and he thrust out his arms at the older boy and pushed him on to the floor of the room. He knelt across him and with his fists he hit out at his face and chest, over and over, his knuckles slamming into Ben's cheeks and shoulders and neck. Ben squealed, his face screwed up, his eyes closed, his arms warding off Nicky's blows. Then he started to fight back, twisting from side to side, his hips thrusting to try and dislodge Nicky. This sent Nicky into a fury and he began to scream himself, drowning out the older boy's cries.

The blood made him stop. It was the deepest red he had ever seen; it bubbled out of Ben's nose and mouth and shocked him into stillness. He climbed off Ben just as the door opened and Helen and Patrick stood there.

'What on earth?' Helen said.

'What's happening?' Patrick said, his voice lower than his wife's, his eyes darting round the room, finally resting on Nicky. Ben was still lying on the floor, coughing, his hands across his bloody nose. Nicky stood tall, staring back at Patrick, his eyes brimming with hatred.

Had Patrick known what was going on? Had he known and done nothing? Was his only concern that Helen shouldn't find out?

Without a word he walked past them and went to his own room and started to pack, tipping out the drawers on to his bed and shoving things into his case and hold-all.

'I don't understand it,' he heard Helen saying to Patrick. 'He was settling in so well. You ask anyone and they'll tell you!'

He'd ignored it all. He sat by the window and waited for Lesley to come. After a while he took a nail and scratched it back and forth across his wrist. The criss-cross lines looked like someone's doodles. It stung fiercely and he found himself gripping his sleeve to dull the pain. It didn't matter though. It took all his attention and he didn't need to think of anything else. When Lesley came she looked closely at him. *What's wrong? What's happened?* she said.

How could he tell her? Embarrassment and shame made him shake his head, shrug his shoulders. What sort of person was he? He was nothing, less than nothing. He left the house with his shoulders rounded. In the car he felt small, as if he had shrunk, as if the seats had got bigger.

Now Nicky pulled the ends of the sleeping bag around his feet. He lay sideways and rested his head on the pillow and watched the candles flickering in the dark room. He wasn't afraid. His hand was throbbing and his throat was dry as dust but that didn't matter. If he could sleep for a while perhaps the bleeding would stop and he would feel better. He lay for a long while, his eyes heavy, his body laden with tiredness, sinking into a shallow sleep.

A sound from downstairs made him sit up groggily.

He listened hard. From the back of the house he could hear someone. He thought of the policeman who had tried the front door. He would be back, of course. It wouldn't take a genius to put two and two together. The police knew that the front of the building was locked up. Most likely they'd decided to try the back. Perhaps they'd gone off to get bolt cutters in case that too was locked.

He felt no panic, no sense of worry. Let them come. He had no energy to go anywhere or do anything.

They would want to know what he thought he was doing. Why he had been camping out in the house across the road and watching Lesley's daughter. What had been his intention? He wouldn't be able to answer. He would look like some kind of nutter. How could he explain? He didn't even understand himself.

He heard a sound like a cough and footsteps shuffling along the downstairs hall. He bit into his bottom lip, imagining the policeman edging along in the darkness. He'd have a torch, no doubt, and was following the circle of light as it rose up the stairs in front of him.

His hand was hurting and he held it close to his chest. They would take him to hospital and under bright strip lights there would be concerned faces. He felt a sudden longing to be there among the doctors and nurses; to be looked after, bandaged up and cared for.

The footsteps had reached the top landing. They were slow and careful; Nicky imagined the policeman searching the floor with his light to make sure that it was safe to walk on the boards. More than likely there was another reason for the caution. The policeman may think that Nicky was armed and dangerous. The man may be tensing himself for some sort of attack.

He could see the door handle turning. He wanted to say something, to shout out and reassure whoever it was that it was safe, that he wasn't going to cause any trouble. He even opened his mouth to speak but the words weren't there. They'd dried up. Instead, he looked down at his injured hand and saw the blood, like a flower blossoming darkly in his palm. He felt heavy, as though he was going to sink into his sleeping bag; his eyelids wanted to close but he held them open just as the door opened gently.

From the darkness emerged a figure, standing looking down at him.

He'd thought it would be a policeman but it wasn't.

'What's happened to you, Nick?' the voice said.

It was Vince, the boy from Crystal House.

Part Two

Found

19

The bleeding did stop. Nicky was grateful to Vince for that.

'What have you done?' the boy had said when he came into the room.

Nicky could hardly speak. He held his hand out and Vince squatted down in front of him. He took Nicky's hand and looked at the soaked T-shirt. His face was screwed up in sympathy. Then he surveyed the dark room with its flickering lights, narrowing his eyes up to see into the corners.

'This looks bad,' he whispered dramatically. 'You should go to A and E.'

'I can't . . . the police . . .' Nicky gasped the words out.

Vince nodded slowly as though he was taking it all in and understanding exactly what had happened. For a second Nicky wondered what was going through the boy's mind, what kind of scenario he thought had brought this about. Possibly he imagined Nicky had been involved in some major crime; or perhaps some kind of alien visitation. These things were too much for Nicky and the thoughts slipped away from him as he felt the pain in his hand grow bigger until, in the hazy light, he fancied the hand itself had enlarged and was like the giant paw of some animal.

'You stay here,' Vince said importantly. 'I got the picture. I know what to do. You stay here,' he repeated and then turned his back and left the room.

'No, wait . . .'

Nicky's voice was croaking. He didn't want to be alone again. He heard the footsteps receding and lay his head down. He put his hand to his chest and held it with the other one. After what seemed like a long time he fell into a sleep.

When he opened his eyes Vince was there again. He had no idea how long the boy had been gone but the candles were smaller and the surrounding darkness was closer and thicker. He guessed it must have been quite a while. He had returned loaded with things. On the floor in front of him was a First Aid box. In the half-light Nicky could see the words CRYSTAL HOUSE written on it in felt-tip. He also had some bottled water and some tablets, as well as a can of Coke.

'That's for me,' Vince said. 'The rest is for you. Don't worry. I know what to do. I done some first aid at my last school.'

Nicky edged up and held out his hand. He watched hazily as Vince popped two pills out of a sachet. Then he poured some water into a paper cup.

'Take these. Pain-killers. And lots of water. You have to

have fluid when you've got an injury. Lots of it. Otherwise the body gets dehydrated.'

'How did you find me?' Nicky said, swallowing the pills down and sipping the water.

'I followed you. I've been following you for days, from before you left.'

Vince was gently unwrapping the T-shirt, his eyes narrowing with tension. Nicky's arm was limp, his body weak; he couldn't have got up and walked if the house had been on fire. The last layer of cloth was stuck to his skin and Vince edged it off a centimetre at a time. He pulled a tiny torch out of his jacket pocket and shone it on to the damaged hand. The wounds, four of them in all, were gaping amid layers of crusted blood.

'This is not so bad,' Vince murmured. 'These have dried up . . . It's just one of them that's still wet . . . look, see that. There's still a bit of glass in it. That's why it's so sore.'

Nicky could have cried with relief. Instead he lay back and closed his eyes and let the younger boy take over. He felt wet cotton wool and pressure and some pain as Vince edged a small piece of glass out of his skin. He heard Vince mumbling to himself and felt his hand being washed over and over and then a series of sharp, stinging pains and the heavy smell of TCP.

All the while Vince made him drink more water and kept pulling the sleeping bag around his shoulder. Some time later, when his hand felt clean and rested, he heard the sound of things being cleared up, zips fastened, footsteps. And then there was quiet.

When he woke it was daylight. The light was streaming in through the holes in the wood and room was silent. It took a few minutes for Nicky to remember what had happened. He sat and looked round and saw the figure of Vince in a sleeping bag on the other side of the room. Beside him was a hold-all with a jacket lying across it. The boy's eyes opened and he stretched his arms up. Nicky could almost hear his joints cracking.

'How do you feel?' Vince said.

'Better,' Nicky replied, slowly standing up, surveying the burnt-out candle wicks and the crumpled, bloody T-shirt. Bit by bit it was all coming back to him: the dark room, the whirring fan, the girl on the bed. What had he been thinking of? Chloe, in her flimsy skirt, sleeping like a baby. She must think that he was some kind of pervert.

'I'm with you now, Nicky,' Vince said, rubbing his eyes. 'I'm not going back to Crystal House.'

The sensible thing would have been to send Vince back, to force him to return to the home. He could have done it. The boy respected him, he could have persuaded him. But he didn't. In his head he wasn't even thinking about Vince or Crystal House or any of the other things that had upset him. Those things had faded. His mind had been fogged up but now it was crisp and clear. Something was else was forming, filling his thoughts.

'I can come along with you, I've got thirty quid . . .'

He smiled to himself and looked down at his hand, the wounds held together with tiny strips of plaster that Vince must have cut up. His skin was clean and his arm felt light, as though some dragging weight had been chipped away from it.

'We can travel round together. We can be company for each other.' Vince was talking quickly, his voice on the defensive as though he was losing some battle.

None of it was registering with Nicky. He knew what he was going to do and where he was going to go. It had been staring him in the face, ever since he'd received the letter in the blue envelope. He'd just missed it. He'd been so full of fury and rage that he'd overlooked the most obvious course of action.

'We've got to make plans,' he said. 'We're going to Lowestoft.'

'Lowestoft?' Vince struggled out of his sleeping bag, relief written all over his face, as though he hadn't really expected Nicky to let him stay.

'Yup,' Nicky said, a feeling of lightness coming over him.

'How come?'

'That's where I was born. There's someone I've got to find.'

20

Trevor Williams, the Crystal House social worker, came to see Chloe's dad. He produced a brown envelope out of his jacket pocket and took a photograph out of it. He handed it to him. Chloe could see it. It was a head and shoulders shot of Nicky Nelson. She stared at it. In the light of day Nicky looked like any other boy of her age.

'This lad,' Trevor Williams said, stroking his tie, 'was one of Mrs Cozens's cases. She'd placed him with a family and he was there for almost seven months when he made a sudden unprovoked attack on the couple's son. The boy had to go to the hospital. The family didn't want to press any charges.'

Her dad looked puzzled.

'What's this got to do with us?' he said.

'Two days ago he left Crystal House. No one has seen him since. Naturally I had a good look in his room. I found these.'

Trevor Williams put his hand inside the envelope again and pulled out a couple more photographs and placed them face up on the table. Chloe saw herself, in her school uniform, in the street. Her dad's face hardened.

'I'd already met your daughter so when I saw these I realized who it was.'

'This kid was taking photographs of Chloe? Why?'

Chloe picked up the photographs. They had been taken when she wasn't looking. Her dad looked at the social worker with exasperation.

'You think he may be disturbed?' her dad said.

'No . . . The thing is, Nicky has been all over the place and his history isn't that clear. His case notes were never passed on to Mrs Cozens. Then when she did enquire after them it seems they had been misdirected.'

'Could he have had some sort of grudge against my wife?' her dad said, his voice getting louder. 'We had an odd letter a while back. Could this kid have broken into my house? We had a break-in last night! My wife's things were damaged!'

'I can't say. I just thought you should know about the photos. We've contacted the police about the boy's disappearance. That's the usual procedure in these cases.'

'You should have rung me *immediately*. I wouldn't have gone out and left my daughter alone while there was some unbalanced teenager about.'

Trevor Williams was fiddling with the knot of his tie.

'Nicky Nelson is an odd lad, a loner. I'm told that Mrs Cozens, herself, felt quite attached to him. She did quite a lot to piece his records together. Then, of course, she was ill . . .' he said, glancing at his wristwatch.

'Don't let us keep you,' Chloe's dad said tersely. 'We've a long journey ourselves and we ought to get off.'

Trevor Williams brushed his jeans with his hands. 'The whole matter is now in the hands of the senior social worker. I'll let you know if there are any developments.'

Later, getting into the car to go to Lowestoft, Chloe found herself looking up and down the street. She wondered where Nicky Nelson had gone. He had been watching her. Taking photographs of her. It gave her a little chill.

Now people were watching out for him.

Her gran was waiting in her front garden as they drove up. She clapped her hands as they got out of the car. She was wearing black trousers and a black blouse out of respect, she said, for her next-door neighbour.

When her dad left, Chloe told her gran some of the details.

'It was that lad I asked you about on the phone, Nicky Nelson.'

Her gran nodded absent-mindedly.

'He seems to blame Mum for something.'

'He sounds like a right load of trouble,' her gran said. 'I said to Lesley when she took that job, *You'll meet all sorts there, my girl*. I never wanted her to do a job like that. With her brain she could have worked in some high-flying company. Made a good salary,' she said, adding wistfully, 'and maybe a car as well.'

Later, when her gran had stopped fussing over her and gone next door to help Sonia with some of the funeral arrangements, she decided to go for a walk along the front. She needed to wake up, to feel the sea breeze in her hair. She felt as if she'd been tired and sleepy for weeks.

The seafront was still busy with families and young people going to and fro. Chloe walked across the pebbly beach to the edge of the water. She dipped her foot in the sea. *The sea is always freezing in Lowestoft*, her mum had said. *Even if there's a heatwave you can't stay in the sea too long.* She had a sudden image of herself as a small child on one of their day visits to her gran. Her mum was carrying her out of the water wrapped up in a towelling dressing-gown that had a hood. They'd crouched behind a canvas breaker as the wind rushed past, making her feel chilled, the sand blowing up so that it got into her mouth and made her sandwiches taste gritty. Had her gran been there on the beach that day? She couldn't remember.

She ended up at Benjy's, queuing to buy an ice cream. The place was full of teenagers and she watched them elbow and shove each other playfully. Boys and girls were lounging in the tiny booths, their arms around each other's naked shoulders, their sunglasses pushed up on to the tops of their heads. There was smiling and giggling, secret looks and a girl whispering into the ear of a boy, her lips only a breath away from his skin. All the time, the beeping of mobile phones and the silent posturing of the boys, looking out to sea as if they weren't interested in what was going on around them.

Chloe felt a sting of envy. She took her ice cream and sat down at a table outside and looked through the glass at the carefree kids on the inside. How nice that would be. To get up in the morning and just have to worry about what to wear or whether you had enough money to go out with your mates. She had been like that once; one of the crowd, sashaying down the local shopping centre, her arm linked through Lucy's or Jo's, staring hungrily into the windows of designer shops.

Now it was different. She had no interest in those pastimes any more. She'd lost her mum. Clothes, schoolwork, romance, these things were just fripperies; bubbles that would dissolve, pop, or float away. In return for losing all these things she'd found a strange lad who had a grudge against her mum and maybe her too. Perhaps he saw her as some kind of target for his unhappiness. And yet that didn't quite explain his brief relationship with her. His friendliness, his calls, his kiss; him *forcing* himself on her. These things didn't fit. He was like two different people. If only she could find out which was the real Nicky Nelson.

Looking up, she saw her gran walking along the promenade coming towards her. She had taken off her black blouse and trousers and was wearing a floral sleeveless dress. The dogs were on leads and she was carefully sidestepping them when they strayed in front of her. Next to her was Sonia, loosely linking her gran's arm and smiling and pointing in her direction. Chloe was surprised. She had expected Sonia to be in deep mourning, the way she had been when her mum died. But she seemed just like everyone else, enjoying the sunshine and the sea air. Not only that but she looked different, taller, prettier somehow.

'Two Knickerbocker Glories,' her gran said when they reached her.

'Oh Lily, they don't do those any more,' Sonia said, pulling some chairs out for them to sit on.

In the days that followed Chloe filled the time by helping her gran and Sonia prepare for the funeral.

'This isn't painful for you?' her gran asked her. 'Reminding you about Lesley?'

'It's OK. Mum's always in my mind. But in a good way,' she said.

She thought a lot about Nicky. Would she ever have a chance to talk to him about her mum and his grudge? To clear up whatever the misunderstanding was. Whenever she started to feel flaky or lonely or sorry for herself she simply directed her thoughts back to him. A hard determination filled her. She would talk to her dad and sort out the situation. When she remembered him in her room a few nights before it gave her a queasy feeling. She had been alarmed, that was true, but moments later, when he retreated looking dazed and distant, she knew that something was badly wrong with him. If her mum had been there she would have sorted it out. Maybe Chloe could do it in her place.

The fourth morning at her gran's she was surprised to see Sonia appearing in her gran's kitchen looking businesslike, wearing some smart trousers and a blouse. Her hair was up at the back and she was wearing earrings and lipstick. She was holding a grey folder that looked years old. Chloe's gran stood up to give her a hug. After a few minutes of quiet conversation she heard her gran say something like, *You're doing the right thing, my love*. Then Sonia left, giving Chloe a tiny wave.

Sonia seemed more relaxed than Chloe had ever seen her. Her face had a shine to it, a glow that she couldn't really describe. Instead of being washed out and crumpled up as Chloe had been after her mum died, Sonia seemed invigorated. Chloe didn't know what to think about it. She did know that she liked Sonia. She'd watched the way her gran got on with her, how the two of them joked and laughed, how they hugged and gave each other little kisses whenever they parted. It made her feel a little bit sad. She had never seen her mum and gran like that together.

'Where's Sonia off to?' she said.

'The solicitor's. She's got some business things to sort out.'

Her dad had gone to the solicitor's. When someone

died it seemed that papers had to be signed and filed. As though dead people were like parcels that had to go through the system; checked in at one end and stamped out at the other.

'She looks really well!'

Chloe picked up a tea towel to dry the things that her gran was washing up. The water was running into the sink, steam coming off it.

'She does. It's probably not the right thing to say but Sonia will do better now that her mum has finally gone. Her mum was a sweet old lady but she depended on Sonia for everything. Sonia had no life of her own.'

'What about her dad?'

'A horrible man. In the army. Things were always relaxed when he was away but when he came back he ruled with a rod of iron.'

'Why didn't Sonia ever get married?'

'No one was good enough. After her dad died her mum wanted her to marry someone from the church but she never did. Soft as she was, she put her foot down at that. They had a few rows, I can tell you.'

Her gran turned to the sink and started on the dishes. Using a small plastic brush she scrubbed at a plate and then held it under a running tap until the suds had disappeared.

'Gran, how come you and Mum fell out? How come you didn't see each other for five years?'

The words just came out. She hadn't meant to ask.

It seemed like such an enormous question; five years of silence.

'What was it you rowed about?' Chloe said, softly.

Her gran's face took on a look of mild exasperation as if she was irritated by the question. Then she seemed to soften.

'We had words,' she said, pulling the plug out of the sink. The sound of the water draining away filled the quiet room. 'About Sonia. Your mum got to know her over the years and was very fond of her. She didn't like the fact that Vera was so weak and never stood up to Ronnie. It meant that everything had to be done in a particular way. Your mum thought Sonia should have more freedom, maybe think about going away to university. But Vera was always afraid of what Ronnie would say. In the end I had to tell your mum to mind her own business. I didn't mean it cruelly, you know, but Sonia was their daughter. Your mum took it badly. See, she was sticking up for teenagers in those days as well.'

'And that's why she didn't come back for *five* years?'

'That's how it began. But she was stubborn. And so was I. I regret it now, of course. Now that she's gone.'

Her gran pulled the rubber gloves off, shaking them into the sink. Then she took two steps forward and gave Chloe a bear hug, pinning her arms to her side.

'That's all in the past. Better forgotten,' she said, her voice low. 'Now, could you pop next door and put those sausage rolls in Sonia's freezer? Her key's up there on a hook.'

Chloe unhooked a pair of keys, picked up the food and went out the back door and through the gap in the garden fence. The sight of Sonia's kitchen made her pause for a moment. It was from another era. It was crammed with wooden cupboards, none of which matched. A cooker stood on legs in the middle of one wall. It was small; the oven bit didn't even look big enough for a turkey. The only modern appliance in the room was the fridge-freezer. She opened the door and put the food into the trays. Making sure it was properly closed she had a last look at the spin-dryer, the old bread bin, the sink with one tap and a water heater above it. On a small table was an old radio, a huge brown wooden box. Beside it was a shoe box opened and inside an array of writing paraphernalia; two or three pads, some pens and packets of envelopes. A page lay to the side with a list of names on it. Chloe glanced over it. Maybe these were letters Sonia had yet to write. She was about to go when something caught her eye.

Underneath some paper was a packet of blue envelopes. She pulled them out.

She had received two blue envelopes and they had caused her a lot of pain. She remembered the words in the first: *I'm not sorry your mum's dead. She ruined my life.* She shrugged. These envelopes were not the same; the colour a shade lighter, perhaps a little bigger as well. She toyed with them for a moment.

Nicky Nelson sent her those letters. What she didn't know was why. Sighing, she replaced Sonia's blue envelopes and wondered if she ever would really know.

21

The tent cost less than a hundred pounds. Taking into account the fares and some food, Nicky still had over a hundred and fifty pounds left. Out of that he paid for the ground rent on the campsite. Two weeks by the sea. Even if he didn't accomplish much it would be a holiday for him and Vince. A crowded place into which they could both disappear.

Nicky tensed himself as he walked into the campsite office. They didn't need any difficult questions; it was better if they went unnoticed. He found his fists closing as they walked up to the counter and looked at the man standing there. He was about forty, his arms and shoulders muscular as though he worked out. His skin was tanned, like old leather. Nicky spoke quickly, asking for a place to pitch the tent. He left no gaps between his words in case it gave the man a chance to butt in. They'd worked out a story on the way down. The man didn't seem bothered, though, and hardly looked up from the paper he was reading.

'Sixty-four quid and there's a charge if you pay with a credit card.'

Nicky handed him the money.

'Pitch 204. The third field along. Showers and toilets about two hundred metres away. No late parties, no overnight guests, no urinating in the hedges,' he said, and added grumpily, 'Have a nice day.'

Nicky and Vince picked up their belongings and walked away with their receipt. At the pitch, alongside a couple of families with small children, they put the new tent up. It was a tiny nylon affair and had just about enough room for the two of them to lie down. Everything else – eating, washing, standing up straight – would have to be done outside.

This didn't bother Nicky. The tent was somewhere to sleep. He had no intention of spending a lot of time there. As soon as they'd unpacked and unrolled their sleeping bags he zipped up and turned the key in the small padlock. All the while Vince was making himself known to the neighbours.

'Let's go for a walk,' Nicky said.

'We'll keep an eye on your stuff,' a woman holding a small child shouted after them.

'Thanks.' Vince waved regally and Nicky found himself smiling at the boy's ease.

'I'm hungry,' Nicky said.

They bought fish and chips in small plastic dishes and sat on the sea wall eating them with tiny wooden forks. It was a warm day but the breeze was stiff and Nicky was glad he'd kept his sweatshirt on. Vince had his jacket on, as usual. They ate silently: for once Vince was quiet, curtailing the constant stream of chatter that usually came out of his mouth.

It had been two days since Vince had turned up at the derelict house in Warwick Lane. Within hours they'd made preparations for their trip but they hadn't left straight away. Nicky was still recovering and they took their time clearing up his stuff and packing it into the alcove, half hidden by a couple of old planks of wood they'd found downstairs. As long as the house didn't get demolished over the next couple of weeks then he thought his things were safe.

He only took what he needed in his rucksack. His money, some clothes, his sleeping bag, his cross and chain and the blue envelope with Lesley's letter in it.

They caught a coach because it was cheaper. It took a long time, though, and Nicky heard just about every detail of Vince's life story. His mum and dad had split up when he was four. For a while he'd lived with his mum and his older brother. Then his mum met a man called Bobby, who moved in with them. Vince liked him but his older brother didn't. After a while his brother went to live with his dad and Vince was alone with his mum and Bobby. Then his mum had another baby and he'd felt left out. He started to be troublesome and got excluded from school. His mum became pregnant again and so Vince had to go and live with his dad. This didn't last, though, and Vince and his brother ended up in care. The social workers tried to place them together, as a family, but it didn't work out. Vince and his brother weren't used to living under the same roof. Then Vince was placed on his own; twice. He ended up in Crystal House.

'The Mother Ship,' Vince said.

It took a minute for the penny to drop but then Nicky laughed out loud. *The Mother Ship*. It was a good joke.

'Where's your mum now?' Nicky said.

Vince shrugged his shoulders. He still had a smile on his face but it was a frozen expression, just a picture with no feelings behind it. Nicky didn't probe. It was better to let people keep their own secrets. He, of all people, knew that.

The seafront was busy. The cool breeze hadn't put off the holidaymakers. The beach was dotted with families in swimwear, sheltering behind windbreaks. From where he stood it looked like little tribes of people holed up behind walls, only the young ones venturing out with spades and buckets. From the nearby arcades he could hear the cheerful music of the amusements, the clattering of coins and the pencil-thin voice of the bingo caller.

'Who is it we're looking for?' Vince said, posting his empty tray of food into a bin.

Nicky turned towards him. It was a blunt question but he knew Vince wasn't being nosey. The boy had hardly asked him a thing since he first arrived at the house. In the couple of days that they'd stayed there together he'd seemed happy to nip out to the shops from time to time, to wash and change Nicky's dressing, to mooch around the empty building or curl up in the corner just reading his magazines. He hadn't asked why Nicky was there; he hadn't asked how Nicky had injured his hand. He was just pleased to be there with him.

Nicky hadn't said much throughout. An explanation was a big task; like writing a story. It had to have a beginning, a middle and an end. The beginning he knew; the middle he was experiencing; the end was unpredictable. He stood up.

'Let's go on a trip,' he said, brushing crumbs from his jeans. 'I want to show you a church.'

'Church?' Vince said, looking puzzled.

'Tell you why when we get there,' Nicky said, studying the palms of his hands, one covered in sticking plaster, the other red and sore-looking.

Great Yarmouth was ten miles or so up the coast. They caught a bus and after about twenty minutes they stepped off into a much bigger seaside town altogether. The front stretched as far as the eye could see, the beach was full of families and bathers and there were speedboats and windsurfers further out on the sea. It was noisy as well; the nearby funfair pouring out music into the street, the squeals of people on the rides travelling through the hot air, the sound of car horns beeping in the congested traffic.

As soon as the bus moved off Nicky walked in the

direction of the Tourist Information office. Vince waited outside and Nicky emerged moments later with a map.

'It's not far,' he said.

'What church is it?' Vince said curiously.

'St Nicholas's.'

If Vince attached any significance to the name he didn't comment. They walked along, sidestepping other people, half on the pavement and half on the road when it got too crowded. Vince followed brightly along as though this had been just what he was expecting to do. Nothing seemed to phase him. He was easy-going, good company. Back in Crystal House there had been a hint of desperation about him and none of the kids had wanted to know. Here with Nicky his true side was coming out.

After a while he started to talk excitedly about religion.

'In the olden days, before people knew about science and space and stuff,' he said, 'people thought that UFOs were gods. Some people think that aliens built the pyramids and the Sphinx. And in Australia, there's an Aboriginal myth that says the world was created by spirits who arrived in flying crafts. See? Spaceships. They couldn't explain them so they called it some sort of religon.'

'But there's no real proof,' Nicky said, pausing to cross the road. 'Otherwise we'd know. It would be reported in the papers!'

'No, because the government keeps it a secret.'

'But, why?'

'To stop panic. Can you imagine if spaceships suddenly landed, like over there?' Vince pointed to the beach excitedly. 'Imagine the panic there'd be.'

'Hundreds of little green men walking along by the amusement arcades.'

'They're not little green men,' Vince said, smiling. 'Look, there are more planets and stars in the universe than grains of sand on that beach. Are you saying that Earth is the only place where there's life?'

Nicky didn't speak. Vince had a point, he had to admit. He *ummed* as he checked the map and they turned off from the seafront and found themselves in quiet residential streets, road after road of brick houses with trees along the pavements.

'You been to this church before?' Vince said, puffing slightly.

'Yes. I don't remember it though.'

They were in Nelson Road. Nicky stopped for a minute and looked at the street name-plate. *Nelson*, it wasn't a bad name. Up in front of them, just visible round a bend, Nicky could see the spire of a church. St Nicholas's. The building was small and modern, with sharp angles and floor-to-ceiling strips of glass. In front there was a notice-board. *Can You Take Christ Into Your Life?* a poster said.

'This it?' Vince said, unnecessarily, as they stood in front of the church wall looking over at a small car park. A large tree stood at the edge, its branches stretching out like a giant umbrella. It looked as though it had been there a lot longer than the church.

'Let's go in,' Nicky said.

He walked through the car park and towards the wooden doors. Inside the church was dark and cool, the benches made of honey-coloured wood. The altar was small and plain, just a table with some flowers and a crucifix.

'Up here,' he said.

They walked up to the front and Nicky slid along the bench in the second row. Vince followed looking mildly uncomfortable. He cleared his throat a couple of times.

'Is this where your mum's funeral was, Nick?' he said finally.

Nicky smiled, looking round the quiet church. The long windows meant that the sun was lying across the floor and the benches, dividing the area up into dark and light. The sound of a door opening made them both look. A woman came in. She wore a white collar and she walked down the middle aisle giving them a pleasant nod as she passed.

'My mum's not dead. I've come here because it's where I was found. Here on this bench. I was three months old and some churchgoer found me here, in a Moses basket.'

Vince opened his mouth to speak but for once he seemed lost for words. His face took on an expression of incomprehension.

'Like ET,' Nicky sighed. 'You know, left behind by his mother.'

Vince nodded slowly as the pieces dropped into place and the words became clear. Nicky turned away. All of a sudden he was too full of emotion to say another word.

Vince was patient, Nicky had to admit that. When he finally understood that Nicky wasn't joking about his birth circumstances, he was carried along in a kind of silent astonishment. He didn't push for information but bided his time until the story was told. It took a couple of hours for Nicky to tell Vince about his life. They sat on the end of the pier while Nicky told it to him in small bits, like episodes of a soap opera. They ate hot sugary doughnuts and drank cans of Coke.

There were things he didn't tell. Things that he would never be able to tell anyone. Ben Marshall, the moody boy with long hair, who was always there in the shadows of Nicky's story. A prickle of shame and hurt rose up in his chest whenever he thought of him but he pushed it down, hid it away. Maybe one day Ben would fade from his thoughts and it would be as though it had never happened.

In any case the bit Vince was most interested in was Nicky's birth story. He kept asking about it over and over. It was like something from a classic myth or legend. A baby, left in a basket, in a church pew.

They caught a bus back to Lowestoft. When they got off the sky had clouded over and it had started to rain. Nicky wanted to find somewhere that they could go and sit. They passed by McDonalds and the amusement arcades. His mood had dipped and he was sick of the noise and crowds of kids and people. He wanted somewhere quiet, where he could think.

'I know,' Vince said, striding off, away from the front.

They came to a library.

'Libraries are all right. I used to go a lot. For research purposes. As long as you don't make a fuss they leave you alone. No one bothers you. They've got internet and street maps and daily newspapers as well.'

They sat at the table that was furthest away from the librarian's desk. Vince took a pad out of his pocket that he'd bought earlier. On it were some notes he'd written. At the top was a date and the name and address of the church. Nicky noticed that Vince had taken his jacket off. It was draped round the back of the chair. The boy looked odd without it, a different shape, his arms thin and long.

'Let's go over it once more and see if there's anything you've missed out,' Vince said.

Nicky rolled his eyes. Vince had some idea that he was going to investigate Nicky's birth. He should have minded or even been irritated. But he wasn't. He liked hearing it talked about.

Some of it he had known for years; the social worker (*call me Barbara*) who'd given him the cross and chain had told him how he'd been found. He was about seven at the time and had been in a room off from her office; a funny place with armchairs and cheerful wallpaper and a

164

television set in the corner. *The Family Room*, it was called. He'd sat on one chair and she'd sat on another.

When he was born his birth mother hadn't been able to look after him properly, Barbara had said. She'd made a decision to leave him there in that church for some other mother to find. She'd left a cross and chain deep inside his Babygro. Her present to him. He'd been almost three months old.

He hadn't been able to take it in. There was a baby in a basket and it had been him. Surely he would have known, he would have remembered?

A churchgoer found him. He was taken into care but his mother never came forward. Your mother loved you, Barbara had said. She just couldn't look after you. That's why she left you in a church so that some decent person would find you.

He'd believed her utterly. In his young mind he'd pictured some woman slipping into the church carrying a baby in a basket. She'd been sad, distraught even, but she'd done it for the best. He'd imagined her placing a kiss on her middle finger and then touching his lips before she looked around and then fled.

How wrong he had been.

'Your mother could have lived in any of the streets surrounding the church,' Vince whispered, looking at the notes he'd made.

'She wasn't from Great Yarmouth. When she gave birth to me she lived here in Lowestoft.'

165

Vince looked baffled.

'I thought you said you'd never met her, that you didn't know her?'

'I haven't met her. But I do know that she still lives in Lowestoft. I also know that it wasn't her who left me in the church but her family. Remember Lesley Cozens? My social worker?'

Vince nodded.

'Well, she knew all about it. She wrote me a letter before she died and told me everything. Here,' he said, pulling the blue envelope out of his pocket and throwing it down on the table in front of Vince. 'Read it.'

22

Chloe couldn't believe it when she saw Nicky Nelson walking along the seafront at Lowestoft. She screwed her eyes up as he disappeared behind a group of people emerging from an arcade. She stood in one spot and watched. She'd been thinking about him a lot and there he was in front of her. She could be mistaken, maybe it was some other similar-looking lad. But when the group moved she saw him standing looking into a shop window with a younger boy. It was Nicky, his dark spiky hair sticking up on the top of his head.

She was momentarily alarmed. She stood behind a tree and folded her arms tightly across her chest. Had he followed her there? To Lowestoft? Should she phone her dad? The police? Trevor, the social worker?

As she watched him her anxiety seeped away. There was something different about him. He was walking along, a spring in his step, and was in conversation with the other boy, who was gesticulating with his hands. Nicky turned his head sideways for a second and she saw that he was *smiling*.

She uncrossed her arms and felt herself relax.

What was he doing here? In Lowestoft?

Keeping him in her sights, she walked along until she saw him stop and sit down. She stood still, standing at a rack of seaside postcards, and pretended to flick through. Who was the other boy? Why was he here? Should she ring someone and tell them?

She knew immediately that she wasn't going to contact anyone.

When they got up to move on she followed them. This is my chance to ask him, she thought. Why had he come into her room and tried to force himself on her? Why had he sent the letter? The photograph? Was it he who had broken her window? This was his chance to give her an explanation.

The two boys walked away from the front. They paused and crossed through lines of traffic, zigzagging between the cars and heading up a side road. She followed, slowing her steps. Off the seafront there were less people about and she was worried that they might turn and see her before she'd really decided what she was going to say.

The boys turned left and were out of sight a few minutes. She hurried her footsteps in case they went into a house somewhere before she caught up to them. She thought about what she would say. She would be calm, ask him to sit down somewhere, explain how much he had upset her. Quiz him with some carefully phrased questions. Try to get him to *open up*. She tutted. She was sounding like a social worker.

She could see a campsite. There were caravans and trailers and what looked like a small village of higgledy-piggledy tents. There was an orange neon sign that flashed on and off saying, *VACANCIES*. The boys turned into the entrance, the younger one glancing back at her.

Even though she had tiny butterflies in her stomach she put a firm foot forward. She'd be straight but gentle. She didn't want to upset him. They walked through the bulk of the tents and caravans and headed away from the entrance. Up ahead were a couple of fields that just had a few occupants; caravans and tents spread out and a small brick-built building the size of a garden shed that said, *Shower and WC*.

She paused. It was only a matter of a few moments now until she came upon them. What if she was wrong? What if he hadn't sent the letter and the photograph and broken the window? What if he was just a disturbed boy who had broken into her house and tried to force himself on to her?

They turned into the first field and headed towards a small encampment of tents, stopping at a tiny one on the edge. The younger one looked back again and then said something. Nicky turned round and saw her.

He was surprised, she could tell. He hadn't expected to see *her* of all people. She stopped in mid-step and then, feeling silly, walked ahead again until she was only metres away from him. As she got closer she noticed him standing tall, his shoulders squaring, his arms stiffening, his head held high. He was all straight lines and uncompromising corners and his face was tipped back slightly as though he was ready for a row.

Part of her wanted to turn away; to walk out of the caravan park and away back towards the sea. But she had things to ask him. He was fiddling with the neck of his T-shirt and she saw the plasters on his hand. It took her back to the night in her room, the French doors open, when he had crept in like a thief and tried to take something from her. It made her suddenly angry.

'Why do you hate my mother? Why did you try to hurt me?'

There. She'd said it. The words came out with an air of confidence that she didn't feel. Nicky's eyelids quivered but apart from that there was no sign that he was affected by her words. The younger boy gave an exaggerated roll of the eyes.

'Tell her, Nick. Tell her about her precious mum . . .'

Her eyes dropped down to his arm where the pink scars were. She needed to know.

'Why?' she said.

'I don't hate your mum,' he said, 'but she did ruin my life.'

They followed Chloe to an ice-cream parlour called Benjy's. Nicky let her walk ahead. Her hair was up on top in that funny ponytail and she was wearing long shorts and a sleeveless T-shirt. Her legs and arms were white, as though she went out of her way to avoid the sun.

He'd been surprised to see her. Astonished. And yet it made sense. Lowestoft. Everything started there. Lesley had told him in her letter.

In the ice-cream parlour the lunchtime rush had gone and the place had the feel of the aftermath of a battle. There were tables that hadn't been cleared and serviettes and wrappers on the seats and the floor. The woman behind the counter looked hot and sweaty; a man in a white cotton jacket with the word BENJY'S on the back was distancing himself by serving at the ice-cream machine outside. A pale teenager was languidly clearing the tables, piling cups and plates on to a trolley and wiping the surfaces with a grimy cloth.

The three of them had cans of Coke and Vince had a packet of crisps. Nicky sat quietly while Chloe fussed about with her can, pouring it into a long glass that had two squares of ice in the bottom. She kept catching his eye and then looking away.

Since the campsite he'd not said much. He'd left it to Vince to do the talking, to explain the situation. And the boy was doing it in a garbled upside-down way, getting the details mixed up and in the wrong order. What could he expect? It wasn't Vince's story. He didn't have every moment of it ingrained in his thoughts.

'I was sorry about your mum's illness,' he said, interrupting Vince.

She looked at him over the top of the glass.

'Really, I was. She was nice to me. Before she got ill, I mean.'

She nodded, her eyes glassing over. Nicky looked down, hoping that she wasn't going to cry. He had an urge to soothe her, to tell her it was all right. He almost put his hand across the table and then he stopped. Why should he care? Look at him, look at his life. He had been the victim, not her. She had had a lifetime of her mother and he had had nothing.

He sat very still for a moment, waiting for the anger, like an express train, to thunder into his chest. The girl, Chloe, seemed to be building up to say something. Let her. What could she say that would make any difference?

'Maybe my mum just did what she thought was best at the time.'

The words crept out of her mouth. Nicky stared straight at her, his chest curiously calm, no sign of his temper, not even in the far distance.

'Do you know how many homes I've lived in?' he said blankly.

She shook her head.

'You've only lived in one home.'

'My mum was a good person . . .'

'She could have been a better person. She told me so in her letter.'

'Can I see it?' Chloe said.

It only took a minute to get out the blue envelope and

toss it across the table. He couldn't read her expression as she picked it up. She examined the envelope for a moment and he remembered, with embarrassment, the things he had sent to her. *I'm not sorry your mum's dead.* He looked down at the table, at Vince's crisp bag which was flat and empty.

After a moment she took out the second envelope and then the letter itself. Sitting back in the seat she started to read.

Nicky could remember every word. He let the words play over in his head. He could almost recall Lesley Cozens's voice.

It was just after Easter and I stayed at my mother's; just before my daughter was born. She had some neighbours who I'd known for years. The daughter was young, fourteen. She was a sweet girl and always looked up to me. Her parents were very strict, churchgoers. Her dad was in the army. Away for a few months then back again. He was a violent man. Everyone knew it but no one did anything. No one wanted to interfere. When I got to my mum's that year there was a local press story that just wouldn't go away. A baby had been found in a basket in a church in Great Yarmouth, just up the coast. Everyone was talking about it. My old friends from the neighbourhood, people in shops; it was on the news, in the local press. The baby was three months old.

Strangely enough, my mother didn't talk about it, brushed the subject away whenever I brought it up.

He could see that Chloe was reading intently, her eyes moving along the lines and then back again. After a few minutes she glanced up at him and then back down at the paper.

'Read on,' he said, remembering the next bit. 'It's all there. The whole story.'

In his head the words seemed to speed up.

I didn't see much of the neighbour's daughter in those first few days. I was told she was ill. I didn't think any more of it. Then we had a barbecue one evening and she came out to see me. She seemed withdrawn, mildly upset. She sat in a chair beside mine and held my hand, her fingers closed tightly over mine. It was odd but I didn't mind.

The next morning I went out for a walk and she followed me. She told me that the abandoned baby was hers. That she had had it at home months before while her father was in Northern Ireland. They'd intended to have it adopted before he ever knew about it. They didn't though. She told me she loved the baby more than anything. It's hard to believe but they kept it a secret from the neighbours. Except for my mother.

Chloe's lips had closed tightly. It must be hard for her, Nicky thought. To read it in her own mother's handwriting. He waited while her eyes seemed to reach the bottom of the page and then scanned upwards again. She looked up at him. Her expression was one of sympathy or shame or sorrow, he couldn't quite tell. He wanted to say something but he couldn't. He remembered the night when he had lain next to her, his arm around her. One minute it had been warm and comfortable. The next he'd been on top of her, forcing his knee between her legs. He chewed at his lip in shame. Some things he'd done he simply couldn't explain.

'Your mum could have done something. It's her fault,' Vince said.

Nicky frowned. Vince had a way of simplifying everything. Even in his darkest moments Nicky knew it hadn't been as straightforward as that. None of it was black and white. He cleared his throat. If anything it was like walking through a grey fog.

'Your mum made a decision,' he said, needing to explain it fully. 'She knew who my mother was. She could have phoned the police.'

Chloe was staring at him, hanging on to every word. He remembered the rest of the letter. *I went straight home*, it said. *I demanded to know the truth from my mother. I insisted that she came forward with me to the police. But she stopped me. She reminded me of the girl's dad and his violent behaviour in the past. The girl, your mother, was only fourteen. I was persuaded to leave things as they were. What kind of a home would a baby have in that house? my mother said. I let it go.*

I should have done something but I didn't. I must take responsibility.

There was a feeling of aggravation inside him. It had arrived late, though, and didn't seem to be going anywhere. He couldn't understand it. Before Lowestoft he'd been puffed up with anger; now he was deflated and felt empty and directionless.

'I've got to go,' Chloe said suddenly. 'I'll come and see you at the campsite later.'

She stood up, knocking her glass to the side so that it almost toppled over. She held out the letter in her fingers, her hand trembling. He took it from her without a word. And then she was gone. The door of the shop hung open in the afternoon heat.

'She didn't like that!' Vince said. 'You told her straight!'

Now she knew the truth about Lesley. He had thought about it for a long time; telling her should have made him feel good, set him free of the worry of it all. But he didn't feel one jot better. He just felt the same. That was the story of his life: stop go stop go. In with this family and that council home; this social worker and that psychologist; this helpful teacher and that caring policeman. He had been surrounded by people who were supposed to care for him; a small boy in a flimsy boat tossed about by the waves and finally flung up on to the beach at Lowestoft.

'Let's go down along to the front. We can play on the machines,' Vince said, a swell to his voice, still buoyed up by the confrontation with Chloe Cozens.

Nicky shrugged his shoulders and let himself be drawn along in the slipstream.

23

Sonia was in her kitchen.

'Hi,' Chloe said brightly.

She was clearing out the cupboards. The kitchen table was half full of jars of stuff, condiments and strange, old-fashioned kitchen utensils. Sonia was wearing what looked like a new pair of jeans and a fitted T-shirt and she looked five years younger. On the side was the battered old grey folder that Chloe had seen her go out with the previous day.

'Cup of tea?' Sonia said.

Chloe nodded. On the worktop was a brand-new kettle. It was stainless steel and shaped like a cone.

'My first purchase!' Sonia said, showing it to her. 'What do you think?'

Chloe nodded enthusiastically. She sat down and looked around while Sonia got out the mugs. On the table in front of her were a couple of college prospectuses.

'Are you going to do a course?' she said.

'Possibly. I might do my GCSEs. I never got the chance. When I was younger . . .'

Sonia was waiting for the kettle to boil, using a tea

towel to polish its surface until it was like a mirror. When it started to steam and then clicked itself off, Sonia looked at her with a self-satisfied expression on her face. She was in good spirits and Chloe felt her courage slipping.

She hadn't run straight from Benjy's and burst in. She'd gone back to her gran's house first to give herself time to calm down. Thankfully her gran was out so there were no questions. She paced about. Was this the right thing to do? To tell Sonia about Nicky? To tell Nicky about Sonia? She sat on her bed and thought of the letter. Her mum had been clear. *I should have done something but I didn't. I must take responsibility.* Her mum wished she had done things differently. Maybe she, Chloe, could put things right.

Sonia gave her a mug of tea and sat down opposite her.

'Your gran's gone to get some cigarettes,' she said and then put her hand over her mouth. 'I shouldn't have said that! You know she's always trying to give them up.'

Chloe smiled nervously. She had no idea how to bring the subject up. Eventually she started talking.

'You and my mum got on well, didn't you?'

Sonia nodded. Chloe focused on an old-fashioned egg-timer that was sitting on the table. It was tightly nipped in at the waist, a small hill of sand in the bottom half, its glass looking smeared and dusty. Minutes and hours and days had passed right through it since the day that Sonia followed her mum and told her about her baby. She couldn't help but see a picture of her mum, pregnant, lumbering along the seafront, and Sonia, a plump girl of fourteen, running up behind her and unburdening her story.

'Do you remember when Mum was here, staying with Gran, just before I was born?'

There was quiet for a minute. Eventually Sonia spoke, her voice sounding husky. 'That was a long time ago.'

Chloe turned to her. It was now or never. She had to tell Sonia about Nicky Nelson.

'I know . . . about the baby,' she said, her words shrinking to a whisper.

Sonia's eyebrows crinkled up. From outside, from somewhere in the street, Chloe thought she could hear her gran's voice calling to someone.

'Sonia, I know you had a baby and that you left it in a church.'

Sonia looked puzzled, 'Did your gran . . . ?' she started.

'No, no . . . Not gran.'

'I don't understand.'

'He was left in a Moses basket, in a church. He was three months old . . .'

Chloe wasn't being unkind. She had to say these things. Sonia would want to know about Nicky, she was sure. In the distance she heard the sound of the dogs barking loudly and the front door of her gran's house banging shut. She was back from the shop.

'I know because my mum wrote it in a letter before she died. You know about that letter, don't you? You sent it to Nicky.'

Sonia looked lost. Then her forehead crinkled and she seemed to tense. She took a deep breath.

'If it were up to me, I wouldn't have left him. You have to understand that. My dad was coming home on leave. Mum said there was nothing we could do. Your gran, she helped. It was for the best, that's what everyone said.'

'I know where he is. I've met him!'

It seemed important to get the facts out in the open so that Sonia could hear them. Chloe had the feeling that if her gran had been there her words would have been sucked up into a file somewhere and Sonia would have missed the truth of it.

'You could meet him. He's here, in Lowestoft . . .'

Sonia stood up suddenly, pushing the chair back at a haphazard angle.

'He was fourteen weeks, not three months. Everybody got that wrong.'

'You could meet him!' Chloe repeated.

Sonia was absolutely still for a moment, as though she'was trying to control her breathing. Then she picked up the tatty grey folder that was on the work surface.

'I know what you're saying but I . . . I think we should wait until your gran . . .' she said, patting the folder.

'I know where he is. I've seen him and I've talked to him.'

Sonia was hugging the old folder. She had a look of fearful wonder on her face and Chloe felt a growing apprehension. It had been right to tell her, she was sure. It would be upsetting, she knew, but wasn't it better to know the truth? From outside, in the garden, she thought she heard her gran's voice calling her name.

Sonia's hands were trembling, Chloe could see, and with her fingers she tried to open up the folder as if she was going to get something. She lost her grip, though, and the whole thing slipped away from her and cascaded to the ground, tipping out some of its contents.

'It's OK, Sonia. It's all right really,' Chloe said, ducking down to the floor to scoop up the bits of paper that had dropped. Behind her she heard the scraping of her gran's shoes along the garden path and the sound of her voice calling, first her name and then Sonia's.

There were letters on the floor, on headed notepaper, from solicitors. In among them were newspaper cuttings; old and yellowed. The largest one was cut from the front page of a local newspaper: *BABY ABANDONED IN MOSES BASKET*.

Chloe held it up, just as her gran walked in through the back door.

'What on earth . . . ?' she said.

Chloe stood up, the scattered papers clasped untidily between her hands. She lay them down on the table next to the jars and the egg-timer. Over on the worktop, there were thin wisps of steam trailing out of the new kettle. Sonia was like a statue, her face frozen.

'What's going on?' her gran said, walking straight over to Sonia and putting her arm around her.

'I know about Sonia's baby. His name is Nicky Nelson,' Chloe said. 'And I know where he is.'

Sonia seemed to smile for just a second and then she broke into sobs.

24

Nicky was in the clubhouse playing at a snooker table. He was looking idly through the window out on to the campsite when he saw her, in the distance, looking puffed as though she'd run all the way from somewhere. He was on his own; Vince had gone off to buy some fish and chips because Nicky was hungry. Since arriving at Lowestoft he seemed permanently hungry. He was potting balls, walking languidly round the table, just minding his own business. No one was bothering him. He liked it like that.

He deliberately wasn't looking when she came into the clubhouse; rather he *felt* her enter and continued focusing along his cue at the ball he was about to pot. He heard footsteps and glanced round to see her coming close. Then he turned back to the table.

'Nicky, I . . .' she started.

He set the cue up again and looked along its line. Just a tap, then the ball should hit its target.

'I need to talk to you,' she said, louder.

He stood back, picking up the square of chalk and rubbing it on the end of his cue. He didn't need to do it but it kept him busy, made it look as if he wasn't too bothered by what she had to say.

'Could we go somewhere . . . ? You know, sit and talk.'

'We did that this afternoon,' he said.

'I've got something really important to say.'

'Important? Like the stuff your mum had to tell me?'

She didn't say anything. Her face went flat, lost any excitement it had had. Nicky felt bad suddenly. She looked as if she was on the brink of crying. This girl. She always looked as if she was going to dissolve into tears.

'I know who your mother is. I've just talked to her,' she said.

Did she want a round of applause? It was on the tip of his tongue to say it but he thought she might get upset again. He rolled his eyes. A few weeks ago he'd resented this dopey girl. Now he stopped himself speaking his mind in case it upset her.

'So?' he said.

'She wants to see you.'

'How come she gave me away?'

'Her mum pressurized her. She was only fourteen. My gran also helped to persuade her. I'm trying to be honest, Nicky. Everyone thought it was for the best, at the time.'

Nicky looked off into the distance. He thought he saw Vince's T-shirt coming along the road. Or he was mistaken. Either way, his stomach was rumbling. He could eat a horse.

'She wants to meet you. Her name is Sonia. She's

thirty-one years old and her mum's just died. The thing is, she was already preparing to make contact with you before I even told her you were here! Yesterday she went to a solicitor's to find out if she had any rights over you.'

'Rights?' Nicky said, bridling back. 'After she dumped me?'

'No, I'm telling it wrong. Look, when my mum was ill she found out who you were. She found out that you, this lad she was looking after, had started off as a baby found in a church!'

'I know,' he said, testily. 'She told me in her letter.'

'She didn't only write a letter to you. She wrote to Sonia as well. In fact she sent *two letters* to Sonia. One for her and one for you. She left it up to Sonia to make the decision whether or not to send yours at all.'

Two letters.

'Sonia re-posted yours. In that funny blue envelope. Look, it's the truth because she told me and anyway I've seen the rest of envelopes. They're exactly the same as the one you showed. She sent it to you. She wanted you to know.'

Nicky shifted about a bit. She was making his mother, this Sonia, sound like a saint.

'She wants to meet you tomorrow. In Benjy's at eleven. I told her I would tell you. She's sent you this.'

Chloe put her hand in the pocket of her shorts and pulled out a photograph. She handed it to him.

He steeled himself to look at it. A head and shoulders

shot of a woman he had never met. She looked young and was smiling at the camera, her teeth a little crooked and her hair dark and thick, cut short, sticking up a little on top.

'It was taken a few weeks ago.'

Nicky looked up. Vince had walked into the pool room. He had a puzzled expression on his face and was carrying a paper bag. Chloe looked round at him with frustration all over her face.

'She wants to see you. She's *desperate* to see you. Tomorrow, in Benjy's, at eleven o'clock. It's your choice. She'll be there. I know she will.'

And she turned and started to walk away. Something was nagging at the back of Nicky's mind. Something he had to say to her. He took a few steps.

'Chloe? I'm sorry about the other night . . .'

'She bothering you, Nicky?' Vince said, cradling the bag that held the food.

At the door she turned back.

'Tomorrow at Benjy's. Eleven o'clock.'

He nodded and watched her go. There was paper rattling in his ears. He looked round and saw Vince opening the fish and chips. He looked down at his hand. He was holding the photo of Sonia. Smiling, with dark hair.

'Shall I put salt on yours?' Vince said.

'No, don't bother. I'm not really that hungry now.'

'Oh. Come on!' Vince said, a hint of exasperation in his voice.

Nicky looked up from the photo. The smell of hot fried food hit him. Vince was holding a chip in midair as though trying to tempt him. Oh, why not. He put the photo in the back pocket of his jeans and took the bag of chips that Vince was holding out.

25

Chloe and her gran sat in the seafront shelter, facing away from the beach. Her gran was smoking, bits of her hair blowing across her face, getting in the way of the cigarette.

'I'll never be able to give these up,' she said.

On the ground in front of them were Prince and Queenie, lying at angles, glancing up at her gran now and then. Chloe didn't comment. She quite liked the aroma of her gran's cigarettes, watching her take one out of its cardboard packet, light it, smoke it, then discard it. It measured out the time that they had sat there waiting.

It was five past eleven and there were three half-smoked cigarettes on the wooden seat next to them. Chloe wanted to go and over and dump them in the bin but she was reluctant to move. Sonia was already in Benjy's. She was sitting at a window table looking out to the sea. Chloe could see her profile. She wondered if Sonia could see them. It wasn't a secret that they were there, watching. Her gran had said that Sonia wanted her there. *Just in case.*

Three little words. *Just in case he doesn't come: just in case he is angry; just in case it turns out badly.*

Then there was Nicky to think about. When Chloe had gone to find him the previous day, after telling Sonia, she had been awash with worry. Had she done the right thing? Would it end happily? For either of them?

Sonia had wanted to know everything about Nicky. How tall was he? What colour were his eyes, his hair? Was he good in school? Did he have a job? Did he have a girlfriend? Did he like football? What did he eat? She'd listened in complete silence as Chloe had relayed everything she knew about him.

Sonia had played with the egg-timer, turning it over and over, watching the sand funnelling through. She'd kept looking over at Chloe's gran, waiting for her to say something. After a while she suddenly got up and filled her new kettle and put it on. Her gran looked at it in disbelief. *Where did you get that?* she'd said, looking grateful for something different to talk about.

Sonia seemed all right. She was tidying up the old grey file, straightening up the pages; she seemed in charge of everything.

'I'll tell him eleven o'clock at Benjy's,' Chloe said. 'That's where you can both meet.'

Closing the kitchen door, she waited for a moment before walking away. *Oh Lily*, she heard Sonia say, her voice cracking up. *Will he want to meet me? After all this time?*

At ten past eleven Chloe began to worry. One of the dogs, Prince or Queenie, stood up against her leg and stared at her. She picked it up and placed it on her lap.

'Perhaps he won't come,' she said to her gran. 'Perhaps he's too angry at Sonia, at my mum.'

Her gran didn't answer. She picked up the other dog and held it close to her chest, her other hand holding her cigarette out.

'Maybe he'll blame me. Your mum did. She blamed me for five years.'

In the distance Chloe caught sight of Nicky Nelson's face. She sat up straight, tension holding her back like a rod. He'd just come out of the turning where the campsite was. He was on his own, walking casually along. He might have been on his way to college or to play football. He looked relaxed. The weight on her stomach lifted. Her gran's voice continued.

'Lesley wanted to go to the police, to the authorities. *That girl needs her baby*, she said. But I couldn't. Your mum hadn't lived here for years. She hadn't heard the screaming rows or seen Vera the next day with her face black and blue.'

Chloe kept her eye on Nicky Nelson all the while her gran was talking. He had slowed down, she thought, although she couldn't be sure. She imagined her mum, only weeks from having her own child, probably too emotional to argue. Sonia, only fourteen, used to do doing what she was told.

A line of old-age pensioners were getting off a coach and she lost sight of Nicky for a few seconds. When she saw him again he had stopped. The coach had reversed into a parking area and the people had dispersed. Her shoulders slumped with dismay as she saw him standing still in the middle of the pavement, his face stricken with indecision.

'We didn't know what they'd called the baby but we did hear that he was put up for adoption almost immediately. Not that it helped me and your mum. She wouldn't speak to me, wouldn't return phone calls. She just cut me off. I thought the baby was in a better place, with a family. Me and Sonia, we both thought that he'd lived with a decent family all of his life. That's what I told Sonia, you see. It's what I honestly thought. Lesley thought the same thing, not that we ever referred to it. When we started speaking after five years it was as though it had never happened. It wasn't until last April when she came up here to see some social worker about a boy in her care that she discovered the truth. I told her to leave well alone but it made her so sad. She said to me that she wanted to put it right.'

Her gran's lips were pursed tightly and she was screwing up her eyes to focus on Sonia who was sitting waiting in Benjy's for her son to arrive. Chloe turned her gaze in the opposite direction. There, by a brick wall, a long face among a crowd of day-trippers, was Nicky. He had come to a full stop.

'Sonia wanted to drop everything and go and find him. I persuaded her to wait. We both knew that Vera didn't have long to live . . .'

Nicky had sat down on a wall and was looking intently

at the ground. His shoulders looked rigid and he seemed oblivious of the crowds of holidaymakers milling around in front of him. Chloe stared at him. She willed him to get up and move on. The cafe was only a minute's walk.

'Do you think he'll go?' her gran said.

Chloe shrugged. More than anything she wished he would. For her mum. But most of all for himself.

26

He'd come this far.

The pavement that had seemed clear a few moments before had become congested. People were disembarking from a coach and getting in his way. They were mostly old-age pensioners; some had white hair and looked fragile; others were dressed up in bright colours with stiff hairstyles and high heels, the men in shirts and ties even though they were having a day at the seaside. They all looked cheerful and it irritated him. He sidestepped a couple and up ahead saw the block of buildings that held Benjy's.

It was gone eleven o'clock. He was late. He tried to speed up but his feet felt heavy and slow. Benjy's seemed further away than it had been a moment before. He stood still for a moment and looked down. His trainers looked battered and scuffed even though he'd tried to clean them. There hadn't been an iron to use so his jogging trousers were wrinkled and so was his T-shirt. He'd showered and washed his hair anyway. He had wanted to make an effort. As though he needed to look his best.

His hand had fresh plasters which had been applied by

Vince that morning. It was healing, he knew. Underneath the dressing the skin would knit together until there was no sign of any wound left.

He took a step forward but felt shaky and so he moved sideways and sat on a brick wall. He felt light-headed. A coach was revving up by the side of the road, heat emanating from it. He could smell the exhaust and a feeling of nausea seeped into his stomach.

Why was he doing this?

Up ahead was the sign that hung from the shop where his mother was sitting waiting. *Benjy's Real Italian Ice Cream.* In the distance somewhere he could hear the buzz of a motorbike, soft at first, then louder. It drilled into his forehead. Here he was on his way to meet his mother for the first time. What if it didn't work out? What if he saw her and all the anger and rage that he had bottled up simply spurted out?

He didn't have to go. He could turn round and go back to the campsite. What would he lose? Nothing. He sat quite still for several moments, his arms and legs feeling like part of the wall; solid, immovable, inanimate. He could just stay there, let the world move past him.

But what about the woman in the cafe? He put his hand into his pocket and pulled out his cross and chain. He breathed deeply, his limbs loosening up, the noise gone from his head. He looked around.

The traffic had cleared and the road was empty for a moment. He saw Chloe Cozens sitting in a shelter across the way. She looked serious and was tugging at her ponytail; as though she knew everything that he was thinking. Behind her the sea was choppy, with boats seesawing on the water. The sky was the palest blue, almost translucent.

Lesley Cozens's words floated into his head. *Don't feel anger towards this girl. She was fourteen and her father was a bully and a brute. Her mother was afraid of what he would do if he found out she'd given birth. They kept you secretly for three months. They couldn't bear to be parted from you. When the girl's dad came home her mother grew fearful. My mother helped her. The girl, your mother, was distraught. That's why she appealed to me. She was in a desperate situation and I didn't help her. I blame myself. I should have done something . . . I'm so sorry.*

Sonia. Her name had a soft sound. It made him feel sleepy. He closed his eyes. *Sonia.* He opened them and looked at the cross and chain in his hand. Barbara Dunn had given it to him when he was seven. The police had found it tucked inside his Babygro. Not tucked but *hidden* inside his clothes. A secret message from his mother who hadn't been allowed to keep him.

That's why he was going to meet her.

He stood up, brushed the dirt off the back of his jogging trousers. He looked across at Chloe and raised his hand to wave at her.

Then he walked in the direction of Benjy's.

A note from the author

A letter can bring good or bad news. I wondered
what it would be like to get a letter that changed
everything in a person's life. And if that letter came
from someone who couldn't be contacted. The boy
in my story has already had a hard life. Will he do the
right thing? Or will he let anger and bitterness take
over? He has that choice. Will he take it?

Anne Cassidy is the author of *Looking for JJ*, *Blood
Money* and *Innocent*. She draws closely on her
background and adolescence growing up in East
London for her novels, and always writes about issues
and characters that are close to her heart. She lives in
London with her husband and son.

The DUFF

Seventeen-year-old Bianca Piper is smart, cynical, loyal – and well aware that she's not the hot one in her group of friends. But when high-school jock and all round moron Wesley Rush tells her she's a DUFF – a Designated, Ugly Fat Friend – Bianca does not see the funny side.

She may not be a beauty but she'd never stoop so low as to go anywhere near the likes of Wesley ... Or would she? Bianca is about to find out that attraction defies looks and that sometimes your sworn enemies can become your best friends...

Funny, thoughtful and written by the author when she was only 17, this novel will speak to every teenage girl who has ever thought they were a Duff.

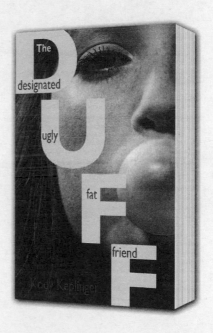

www.hodderchildrens.co.uk

Hodder Children's Books

He's after me

Chris Higgins

'His smile faded and our eyes held. A charge passed through me, like an electric shock.'

Anna meets Jem when her life is falling apart. He is everything Anna needs him to be. Her dad may have run off with a younger woman, her mum may be a wreck and her younger sister, Livi, is swerving off the rails - but as long as she has Jem, Anna will be OK.

And for the first time in her life Anna falls. Deeply and truly and intensely in love.

The end? Not quite...

www.chrishigginsthatsme.com
www.hodderchildrens.co.uk

Hodder
Children's
Books

The day I met Suzie

Chris Higgins

A gritty drama from Chris Higgins about tangled relationships and the danger of manipulation.

'My boyfriend could get into trouble if he gets caught. He could go to jail.' I moan softly. 'So could I.'

'Anything you tell me is completely confidential.' I sigh deeply. What have I got to lose? 'I wouldn't know where to begin.'

'At the beginning?' she says. 'In your own words.'

So that's what I do. I start at the beginning like she says. The day I met Suzie.

www.chrishigginsthatsme.com
www.hodderchildrens.co.uk

Hodder
Children's
Books